FORBIDDEN FRUIT

Other titles available from the *Taggart* series:

Forbidden Fruit

Peter Cave

MAINSTREAM
PUBLISHING

EDINBURGH AND LONDON

First published in Great Britain in 1994 by
MAINSTREAM PUBLISHING COMPANY (EDINBURGH) LTD
7 Albany Street
Edinburgh EH1 3UG

ISBN 1 85158 627 X

A catalogue record for this book is available from the
British Library

Phototypeset in Garamond by Intype, London
Printed in Great Britain by
BPC Paperbacks Ltd, Aylesbury, Bucks

Actor Mark McManus – 'Jim Taggart' to his many millions of fans throughout the world – sadly died during the writing of this book.

He will be greatly missed by all of them.

Chapter One

Joan Mathieson nibbled on her single piece of buttered toast without enjoyment. There was a forlorn, almost resigned look on her thin, pinched features, vaguely reminiscent of a condemned prisoner eating the traditional last meal. Finally, dropping her unfinished toast on to the breakfast plate beside the half-eaten boiled egg, she pushed her chair back from the kitchen table and stared morosely across the room at the two cheap and battered old suitcases which waited, ready-packed, beside the door. She was not looking forward to the journey in front of her, any more than she was prepared to enjoy arriving at her destination.

The honking of a car horn from outside snapped her attention back to matters in hand. Carrying the breakfast plate across the cottage kitchen towards the sink, Joan scraped the unfinished food into a small plastic bag and washed the plate and egg-cup carefully before putting them onto the drying rack. Picking up the food bag, she carried it to the door and out to the dustbins in the small back yard.

She looked across at the ruddy face of her nearest neighbour, Ernie Watt, who stood beside his battered old Land Rover, waiting for her.

'I'll just be a minute,' she told him.

Returning to the cottage, she cast her eyes around the small, neat kitchen to check that everything was ready for her departure, then walked out into the hallway to put on her coat. Pausing only by the hall mirror for long enough to pat her grey, tightly bunched hair into place, she returned to the kitchen and dragged the two suitcases out of the door.

Ernie rushed over to help her. 'I'll take those for you, Joan,' he muttered, smiling good-naturedly. Hefting up the two cases, he carried them across to the Land Rover and placed them in the back.

Joan followed him over to the waiting vehicle, opening the passenger door and climbing in. She sat, stony-faced, staring out of the side window at the whitewashed cob walls of her Perthshire cottage, wondering rather miserably how long it would be before she saw it again.

Ernie clambered in beside her, grinning reassuringly as he saw the look of despondency on her face. 'Aw, come on now, Joan – don't look so miserable,' he chided her, in his broad countryman accent. 'You're going to see your daughter – and to welcome a new grandchild into the world. You should be happy, even if you do have to go to the big city to do it.'

Joan smiled thinly, responding to him. He was

right, she realised. Cathy and the expected baby were the important things. Everything else didn't really matter.

Ernie crunched the gears into place and prepared to move off. 'We'll make your bus with plenty of time to spare,' he assured her. 'Although I don't know why that well-off son-in-law of yours couldn't have come down to pick you up in that fancy car of his.'

Joan said nothing, unhappy to have the subject of Martin brought up at all, and certainly not wanting to talk about him. Perhaps sensing her feelings, Ernie lapsed into silence and began the drive to the bus-stop.

The thunder of city traffic assaulted Joan's ears after the quietness of the countryside. She looked around the busy Glasgow bus terminal almost fearfully, glancing up at the overhead clock for perhaps the twentieth time since she had arrived, a full fifteen minutes ago. She had expected her son-in-law to be there to meet her, at least. Their relationship might be cool to the point of frostiness, but there were certain basic courtesies in life which were common even to high-flying big-city architects with grand ideas and even grander manners.

Finally, with a start of surprise and a feeling of dismay, Joan recognised the heavily pregnant figure of her daughter waddling through the crowded bus station towards her. She looked flushed, out of breath.

'Sorry I'm late, Mum. I got caught in a terrible traffic jam on the Great Western Road.' Cathy leaned over to kiss her mother lightly on the cheek, then bent down with some difficulty to pick up the two suitcases.

Joan knocked her daughter's hand away almost roughly, her eyes blazing with anger. 'You shouldn't

9

even be driving in your condition,' she snapped. 'Couldn't Martin have come?'

Cathy forced a smile. 'You know how busy he always is, Mum. Right now he's got a really tight deadline to meet. He's been working night and day for the past eight weeks. Besides, doctors these days say expectant mothers should keep fit and healthy.'

Joan was unconvinced. 'These days,' she hissed, dismissively. 'I delivered a thousand babies in my time, as well as having four of my own – and there are some things that never change, Cathy. A pregnant woman needs rest, to take things easy.'

Cathy retained her forced smile, unwilling to pursue an argument. She allowed her mother to pick up her suitcases and nodded across the road. 'Come on, then. The car's only over there, anyway.'

She led the way over to the silver-grey BMW, which was parked on a double yellow line. A traffic warden was just closing in for the kill as the two women approached. Noting Cathy's advanced condition, he smiled at her understandingly and put away his notebook.

Helping her mother to load the suitcases and then ushering her into the car, Cathy managed to insinuate herself behind the wheel and drove off.

The large detached house was individualistic almost to the point of ugliness, with lots of irregular angles and much use of glass panelling. It was an architectural statement rather than a family home, appearing to be completely lacking in warmth. Joan Mathieson regarded it miserably, feeling a renewed pang of nostalgia for her own little Perthshire cottage.

'Well, what do you think of it?' Cathy asked. 'Martin designed it himself. He's very proud of it.'

Joan was silent, but her disapproving expression spoke volumes. With a faint sigh, Cathy let it pass. She helped her mother out of the car and led the way up the long drive to the front door, unlocking it.

There was no hallway as such. Apart from a small vestibule, the front entrance let straight in to a huge, open-plan living area which was dominated by a centrally situated open fire and a huge, three-dimensional piece of modern art which took up most of one wall. Again, it seemed to have been designed entirely for visual effect instead of comfort. Glass was again much in evidence in the form of a huge conservatory leading through to the rear of the house, and what few pieces of furniture there were all looked somewhat futuristic and purely functional in design. The general effect only heightened Joan's sense of alienation. In fact, the only object in the room which looked even vaguely homely was a pram – and even that familiar object caused Joan's heart to sink. She turned on her daughter with a shocked, even frightened expression on her face. 'You haven't brought the pram into the house already? Before the baby's born?'

It was an old, meaningless superstition. Cathy dismissed it with a faintly chiding smile. 'Mum, don't be so old-fashioned.'

Joan shook her head slowly from side to side, her expression reproving. 'It's bad luck,' she warned, direly.

'I'll just go and tell Martin you're here,' Cathy announced. 'Make yourself at home.' She disappeared in the direction of her husband's study, leaving Joan to gaze miserably around the cold sterility of the house. Hoping to see at least a bit of comforting greenery, she moved in the direction of the conservatory as Cathy left the room.

Martin Adams was at his drawing board, totally engrossed in his work as Cathy walked in. He glanced up with a look of faint annoyance on his face, upset more by the arrival of his mother-in-law than by the fact of being disturbed. 'So – she's here, then, is she?' he demanded in a peevish tone. 'I suppose that means we'll be having bat soup for dinner tonight.'

Cathy gave him a playful slap on the side of the head, then wrapped her arm around his shoulders and hugged him. 'Try to make an effort, darling,' she murmured in his ear. 'Be nice to her.'

The doubtful look on her husband's face showed that he regarded this as a pretty tall order. Nevertheless, he shrugged philosophically as he rose to his feet. 'I'll try,' he promised. 'But is she going to be nice to me?'

Reassured, Cathy slipped her hand into his and began to lead him towards the confrontation like a lamb to the slaughter.

Joan was peering through the glass doors of the conservatory as they re-entered the lounge area. She jumped back suddenly, letting out a small squeal of fright as a huge, brightly coloured butterfly fluttered in front of her face. Too late, Cathy remembered her mother's strange phobia. Cursing herself for her stupidity, she rushed across to the shivering woman and hugged her comfortingly, pulling her away from the glass doors.

'Oh mum – I'm so sorry,' she said miserably. 'I should have warned you. Tropical butterflies are Martin's hobby.'

Joan was struggling to pull herself together. She glanced up at her daughter with real terror in her eyes.

12

'They can't get into the house, can they?' she asked, in a weak and nervous little voice. 'You know how I hate those things fluttering around.'

Martin hastened to reassure her. 'It's all right,' he promised. 'They need a constant temperature, so it's a sealed environment.'

Joan seemed partly mollified by this information. She allowed Cathy to lead her over to one of the modernistic sculptured easy chairs and sank down into it. Surprisingly, it was a great deal more comfortable than it looked. She began to relax slightly.

Martin moved in the direction of the cocktail bar built against one wall and picked up a couple of glass tumblers. 'Would you care for a drink, Joan?' he enquired in a polite voice, keeping his promise to Cathy to try to be friendly.

It was a wasted gesture. Joan glared at him, her face grim and disapproving. 'Not at midday,' she said, curtly.

Martin took the hint, hurriedly dropping the idea of pouring himself a stiff whisky bracer. He glanced discreetly at his wife, rolling his eyes in a gesture of pained exasperation. If these first five minutes were anything to go by, then the next few weeks were going to be murder, he reflected miserably. It was a savagely ironic and prophetic thought.

Trying to take the edge off the situation, Cathy attempted to cheer her mother up with some good news. 'Ian and Uncle Tom are coming over tomorrow for your birthday,' she announced brightly. She had expected her mother to be pleased, but she was to be sadly disappointed. As ever, Joan chose to see the more negative side of things.

'They could have been here to greet me today,' she

pointed out bluntly. 'But then that's families for you. They all grow up and leave you.'

Chapter Two

The doorbell rang, and Jim Taggart rose from his easy chair to answer it with a slight frown on his craggy features. Evening callers at the Taggart household were unusual, even rare. As rare, in fact, as Taggart himself being in the house before nine o'clock at the earliest.

With his usual guarded curiosity, Taggart glanced out of the window at the vehicle parked outside the house before going to the door. He cared less for surprises than he did for unwanted visitors, and any degree of forewarning was a distinct advantage.

However, the rather flash-looking Japanese 4 × 4 outside the front gate was not familiar to him. Nor did the obviously personalised number-plate PL1 mean anything at all. He moved to open the door, prepared for the worst.

In fact, the surprise was a pleasant one – although a surprise nevertheless. Taggart's jaw sagged open as he recognised the tall, smartly dressed figure of Peter Livingstone standing on his doorstep.

Livingstone smiled at him sheepishly. 'Yes, I know it's been a long time,' he said, apologetically. 'Hello, Jim.'

Taggart continued to gape at him. 'Peter – I don't believe it,' he managed to mutter finally. 'Well, don't just stand there – come on in.' He stepped back, welcoming Livingstone into the hallway. 'Jean will be thrilled to see you,' he added, leading the way down the hall. 'Come on through to the kitchen.'

Livingstone followed him as he threw open the kitchen door with something of a grand flourish. 'You'll never guess who just dropped in,' he announced. Jean Taggart looked up from preparing the evening meal as Taggart led their visitor through the door. Her eyes lit up in welcome. She turned her wheelchair away from the work surface to face him directly, smiling with almost maternal affection.

'Hello Jean – good to see you,' Livingstone said, with genuine warmth. He moved towards her, stooping over to kiss her on the cheek. He turned back to Taggart. 'So, how are you?'

Taggart shrugged. 'Aw, we're doing okay.' He paused, eyeing up the self-assured mature man who stood in front of him, and remembering the somewhat gauche, hesitant young copper who had come to him fresh from police training school and stayed on as his assistant until making detective sergeant. 'So – how long has it been, Peter? Nearly four years?'

Livingstone smiled ruefully. 'Over five, actually. Anyway, how are things at Maryhill these days?'

Taggart grinned rogueishly. 'Since you left, great. The clear-up rate has almost doubled.'

Livingstone took the sarcasm in good heart. He'd expected something along those lines. 'I see you haven't lost your scintillating wit,' he observed.

Taggart grinned again. 'I never found it to start with. Here, let me get you a drink.' He crossed to the kitchen cupboard and took out a bottle of Glenmorangie single malt, pouring two healthy measures.

'We heard you left the force soon after you transferred out of Glasgow,' Jean said. 'What are you doing now, Peter?'

Livingstone visibly preened. 'Actually, I'm running my own security consultancy in Edinburgh,' he announced proudly. He reached into his pocket, pulling out his wallet and opening it to draw out a visiting card and a small sheaf of photographs. 'There's my card,' he said, handing it to Jean. 'And this is a picture of my wife, Marta. She's Portuguese. We got married secretly, on holiday in the south of France.'

Taggart returned with the whiskies. 'You got *married*?' he demanded, as though it was the most unlikely thing in the world. Handing Livingstone his drink, he took the photo from Jean's fingers and appraised the attractive young woman it depicted. He was favourably impressed, but he wasn't going to show it. 'Portuguese wife, eh?' he grunted. 'You always did like to be different.' He caught a baleful glare from Jean, and relented. 'She's a lovely woman. Congratulations.'

Livingstone produced another photograph. 'And this is our son. He's nearly three months old.' He paused. 'Actually, he's the reason I've come to see you.'

'Lost him already, have you?' Taggart queried sarcastically.

Livingstone couldn't help smiling. 'Actually, we're having him christened soon, and I came to ask you both if you'd like to be his godparents.' He watched Taggart's face uncertainly, not quite sure what reaction he was going to get. In fact, the older man was temporarily at a loss for words. He looked touched, almost embarrassed.

Jean answered for them both. 'We'd love to,' she said, delightedly. 'Wouldn't we, Jim?'

Taggart recovered his composure. He nodded emphatically. 'Of course.' He studied the photo more closely. The baby was bonny, sure enough – and showed distinct traces of his mother's good looks, although Taggart failed to find much of Livingstone in him. 'What are you calling the wee fellow?' he asked.

'Xavier,' Livingstone answered proudly.

There was a moment of stunned silence, as Taggart struggled to keep a straight face. Finally, he nodded thoughtfully. 'Xavier, eh?' he murmured. 'Now there's a name that ought to go down well in Edinburgh.'

Martin Adams sat rock-still in the conservatory, surrounded by his beloved butterflies. He held a mushy, over-ripe peach in his hand, allowing the delicate creatures to feed from it, dipping their thin tongues into the dripping nectar as he regarded them with a sense of wonder and unusual peace. It was the one place in which he could really relax and switch off from the pressures of his demanding work. The conservatory was his sanctuary, his own private little Garden of Eden.

The hermetic doors hissed faintly as Cathy came in, breaking the mood. Disturbed by the sudden intrusion, the feeding butterflies fluttered away with a flash of their brightly coloured wings. Martin looked up at his wife, trying to keep the disappointment from showing on his face. As if fending off a potential criticism, he smiled apologetically. 'I thought I made a pretty good effort to be nice to her,' he said defensively.

Cathy nodded. 'She's just lonely, and getting old. She doesn't really mean to be such a shrew.'

It was a judgment which Martin severely doubted, but he let it pass. 'Perhaps she'll be happier when the baby arrives,' he suggested.

The reference to the baby was the cue Cathy had been hoping for. She sat herself down beside Martin on the rocky wall of a bubbling mud pool, clutching at his arm. He glanced sideways, sensing that she had something on her mind from the pressure of her fingers. Cathy's face was serious, troubled. 'About the baby, Martin. I want to tell Mum the truth.'

Martin's features clouded over. 'Do we really have to go into that?'

Cathy nodded. 'I've thought about it a lot, Martin – and I think we have to tell her. After all, Ian and Uncle Tom know, and if one of them said anything and she found out, then I'd feel awful.'

Martin looked totally despondent now. 'And how the hell do you think I feel?' he demanded miserably. 'Everyone in your family knowing?'

Cathy squeezed his arm. 'Come on, love – it's nothing to be ashamed of.'

Martin let out a short, bitter laugh. 'Nothing to be ashamed of? My wife is carrying another man's child because I'm not up to fathering one myself? See reason, Cathy.'

Cathy had not expected quite such a violent reaction. She regarded her husband almost accusingly. 'I thought we'd gone all through this – we discussed it together and with Dr Millar. He warned you that you might feel this way and you promised me that you would resist it.'

Martin jumped to his feet, his anger rising. 'Well, Dr Millar wasn't aware that you were going to blab it out to your uncle, he was going to tell your brother and now, because of it, your mother has to know as well.'

Tears pricked out in Cathy's eyes. She had never been able to cope with Martin's quick temper. It was the one factor which soured their otherwise perfect marriage. She got up, turned away from him and began to walk towards the door before the tears really started falling.

As ever, Martin's fury subsided as fast as it was aroused. He ran to her, embracing her from behind and running his hands over her distended belly. 'He's our baby,' he murmured soothingly in her ear. 'And I'm going to love him to death.' He held her for a few minutes more, preparing himself as much as comforting his wife. 'Well, there's no time like the present,' he muttered eventually. 'Let's get it over with.'

Joan Mathieson was in the kitchen, busying herself with trivial chores which didn't really need doing. It was the one room in the house in which she could feel even vaguely at ease, although the array of gadgets and labour-saving devices both baffled and irritated her. Cathy approached her mother tentatively, as Martin went to pour himself a drink.

'Mum, there's something I've got to tell you – about the baby,' Cathy started, hesitantly.

Joan glanced up, her eyes narrowing slightly. 'What's that?'

'The fact is, Martin and I went to a fertility clinic,' Cathy blurted out, getting it right out into the open.

Her mother looked rather blank. She wasn't quite sure what Cathy was leading up to. 'Oh yes?'

'The thing is – I conceived the baby by A.I.D.,' Cathy went on. 'That's artificial insemination by donor.'

Joan still looked puzzled. 'What exactly are you trying to tell me?' she wanted to know.

Cathy shrugged. 'Well, that's it, really. The donor remains anonymous so we will never know who the father is. As far as we're concerned, it will be our child.'

Joan's expression passed from puzzlement into shock, and finally to one of measured disgust. 'Are you telling me that this baby isn't Martin's?' she asked finally, coldly.

Cathy could only go on the defensive. 'We had been trying for such a long time, Mum. The doctor at the clinic said it was the only way.'

Joan shook her head suddenly, as if to shake what she had just learned out of her mind. 'You've got another man's baby inside you?' she spat out, as though it was something obscene.

Martin entered the kitchen, a glass of whisky in his hand. He slipped one arm around Cathy's waist, backing her up. 'It happens to lots of couples, Joan. We talked about it for ages before deciding – and we're both happy about it.'

Joan turned on him with a look of loathing on her pinched features. 'It's unnatural,' she said disgustedly. 'How can you even think of bringing up another man's child?'

Cathy looked at her mother with a pleading expression in her eyes. 'Please try to understand, Mum. We don't think of it as another man's child. It's our baby.'

Joan shook her head again. She could not, would

not, accept it. 'I brought four of you into the world without having to go to any clinic to have some other man's . . . stuff . . . put inside me.'

Martin was fast losing his temper. 'Well maybe you didn't have the problems we had,' he said curtly.

'Don't you talk to me about problems,' Joan spat, dismissing him. 'And I brought all my children up single-handed.'

'This is different, Mum,' Cathy said miserably, feeling for her husband.

'You could have adopted,' Joan pointed out, flatly. She turned her attention, and her scorn, back on Martin. 'And if you were even half a man, you wouldn't have put my daughter through something like this.'

This final insult snapped Martin's already frayed temper. His face flushed with rage as he threw the glass in his hand to the floor, where it shattered violently. With outstretched fingers, he lunged towards his mother-in-law, as if to seize her round the throat and throttle her.

Cathy screamed, throwing herself between them as her mother backed away with sudden fear showing in her eyes. 'Martin – Stop it! Get hold of yourself!'

Martin's face was contorted with rage. He seemed beyond reason. For a moment, it almost appeared as though he was ready to physically assault his pregnant wife just to get at the object of his fury.

'Please, Martin!' Cathy screamed again, her voice rising to the point of near-hysteria.

Martin seemed to check himself with a visible effort. He stiffened, his whole body trembling. Fists tightly clenched, he stood like a statue for a few seconds before slowly backing away to prop himself up against the kitchen worktop. 'Just get her out of here,' he hissed at Cathy from between clenched teeth. 'Just get her out of my sight before I kill the old witch.'

Chapter Three

There was something going on in the outer office, Taggart realised. Something which for some strange reason caused a buzz of conversation, the sounds of much scraping of chairs as various members of staff got up from their desks to congregate in a small knot which Taggart could see as a misty, moving blur through the frosted glass of his own office door. Stranger still, it was something which was causing DC Reid to make odd little cooing noises, like a slightly muted broody hen.

Whatever it was, it merited investigation. Taggart got up from his desk, crossed his office and threw open the door. He was just in time to catch Jardine's muttered warning. 'Uh oh – now there'll be trouble.'

The knot of people flew apart as the various station staff scurried back to their desks, revealing the centre of attraction which had caused so much disruption. Taggart's scowl evaporated like morning mist in the sunshine, to be replaced by a beaming smile as he recognised Peter Livingstone, his lovely young wife, and their baby. He strode over towards them, blissfully unaware that Jardine was gaping at his unusually benign features with a look of sheer disbelief on his face. 'Peter – you've brought your family in to see me. What a pleasant surprise,' Taggart said warmly. He turned his smile on Marta, waiting for Livingstone to make the introductions and politely shaking her hand when he did so.

'So, you are this Detective Chief Inspector Jim Taggart,' Marta said, with just the faintest trace of a continental accent. 'Peter has told me so much about you.'

Taggart grinned, winking at her. 'Oh, I'll bet he has,' he muttered. He turned his attention to the baby she was holding in her arms. 'So this is the little fellow?'

'What's he called?' Jackie Reid wanted to know.

'Xavier,' Livingstone told her. The announcement was an instant conversation-stopper, with several somewhat embarrassed glances being exchanged.

Taggart's scowl returned. He treated everyone except Livingstone and Marta to a good, warning dose of it. 'What's the matter,' he growled aggressively. 'Have none of you seen a baby before?' His expression softened again. 'Mind if I hold him?' he asked Marta, almost nervously.

'Of course.' Marta handed over the baby into Taggart's outstretched arms.

Jardine and Jackie Reid exchanged a swift, secretive and silent glance which spoke volumes. Now they had seen everything, they both thought. Life would never be quite the same again.

'Careful, sir – make sure you don't drop him,' Jardine put in, half-jokingly.

Taggart turned on him with an expression of scorn. 'This is my *godson* you're talking about.' There was more than a trace of pride in his voice. He continued to rock the baby in his arms as the small crowd began to build up around him again – this time attracted more by the novelty of Taggart in paternal mode than by the baby itself.

The attraction had also proved irresistible for Detective Constable Rob Gibson, Maryhill station's newest recruit and recent first-time father. He hovered behind Peter Livingstone, peering over his shoulder at Taggart. 'What's all this, then?'

'An outbreak of christenings, it appears,' Jardine put in. He looked at Livingstone, offering an explanation. 'This is DC Gibson. His new baby is being christened on Sunday too.' He looked back at Gibson, completing the introductions. 'Peter Livingstone and his wife, Marta. Peter used to be with us. Before he went on to higher things, of course,' he added, in a slightly sarcastic tone.

As Livingstone turned his head to acknowledge Gibson, their eyes met for the first time, and there was a sudden, very strained, moment of recognition which passed between the two men. It was almost as if they shared some deep and dark secret from the rest of the world, and both felt slightly guilty about it.

Seeing the slight frown which passed over Livingstone's face, Jardine mistakenly took it for a reaction to his last comment. Taggart, still revelling in the sensation of holding a baby in his arms after well over twenty years, was totally oblivious to the moment of tension.

Without a word, Gibson turned away abruptly and returned to his desk.

Marta stepped forward. 'Shall I take him now, Chief Inspector?' she offered.

Taggart snapped back to reality. With obvious reluctance, he handed the baby over again. 'Aye, I suppose you'd better. I've got work to do.' With one last look at young Xavier, he turned on his heel and returned to his office.

Jackie Reid tugged at Jardine's sleeve, pulling him away to the sidelines. 'Well, there's one for the record books,' she whispered. 'The old man's got a soft spot after all.'

Jardine looked sideways at her. 'There ought to be a law against it,' he observed quietly.

'What – bringing babies into police stations?'

Jardine grinned. 'No, calling a kid Xavier. I ask you – Xavier Livingstone. What a handle to stick – ' A warning dig in the ribs from Jackie made him break off sharply as Peter Livingstone came up behind them, lighting up a large and expensive cigar with something of a grand gesture.

'So, you finally made it to Inspector,' he said to Jardine. The apparently innocuous statement slid under Jardine's skin like a rapier point, greased with oily, deceptive charm, but carrying a barb.

Jardine's eyes glinted momentarily beneath a polite smile. Livingstone might have drawn first blood, but he was not prepared to let him get away with it. 'I heard through the grapevine that you got passed over for promotion,' he murmured conversationally. 'That's why you quit the force.'

Livingstone parried the returned thrust. 'Lure of private enterprise,' he countered. 'The pull of the '80s.'

28

Jardine had one last stroke up his sleeve. 'I always thought that security companies were something old coppers formed after their retirement.'

Livingstone allowed himself the thin, satisfied smile of victory. 'And I always thought that a university education was totally wasted on you lot,' he observed. Turning away, he returned to Marta and the baby.

Jardine was quietly seething, much to Jackie Reid's amusement. She could sympathise with Jardine, but she didn't really feel sorry for him. Men lacked the subtlety it required to play such games. 'And I thought it was *women* who were supposed to be bitchy,' she observed, flashing Jardine a superior little smile.

Chapter Four

It was all a farce, Martin Adams reflected moodily. A sick, stupid game into which he had been manipulated, unwillingly, into playing a part. But the name of this particular charade was Happy Families, and for the sake of his pregnant wife, he was forcing himself to act out the role which had been thrust upon him.

The little family reunion had been purely Cathy's idea and Martin had gone along with it, although he bitterly regretted it now. It was hard enough to even tolerate the presence of his acid-tongued mother-in-law in the house, let alone make a pretence of enjoying her birthday.

But it was done now, and he had no choice but to make the best of it. Martin ran his eyes over the familiar trappings of celebration. They were all there – the greetings cards with flowery designs and even more flowery, cloying words of false sentiment. The birthday cake – discreetly adorned with only a dozen small candles. And the family members, dragged in under sufferance and forced to play their own roles in the stupid game.

Martin studied closely Cathy's younger brother, Ian, and her Uncle Tom. Both had the same fixed, resigned smiles on their faces, suggesting that they would be as relieved as he would when it was all finally over. Joan Mathieson herself looked equally miserable, as though she was aware of the strained atmosphere in the room. Only Cathy showed any outward signs of enjoying the party – although there was tension behind her smile, knowing that the brittle veneer of bonhomie might be shattered at any second. Martin wondered briefly whether the rest of the family had any genuine affection for the old battle-axe, whether they just tolerated her, or if they actually hated her as much as he did.

Joan was watching a video sent over from Australia by her eldest son and his family. Martin busied himself preparing drinks as the TV set poured out the gushings of goodwill from son, daughter-in-law and three grandchildren. They could afford to be in good spirits, Martin thought resentfully. They were far enough away to be shot of the old bat for ever. He poured whiskies for Tom and Ian and carried them over, just as the video was coming to its predictable conclusion. '. . . Anyway, Mum – you must come over and visit us some time. You know we'd all love to see you. Happy Birthday again. Goodbye.'

The video flickered off into crackling bands of static. Cathy thumbed off the set with the remote control. 'Didn't they all look well?' she asked her mother. 'All so sun-tanned and fit-looking?'

Joan nodded without great enthusiasm. 'And smart,' she observed. She glanced over at Ian, eyeing him with disapproval. 'Not like you, with that scruffy mop of hair.'

Ian frowned. 'I like it this way,' he protested.

Joan dismissed him with a contemptuous sniff. 'All I can say is it's a good job your uncle employs you. If he didn't, no one else would give you a job I'm sure.'

Cathy jumped in again, hastily changing the subject. 'Did Uncle Tom tell you about the new cemetery contract they've got?' she asked her mother. She flashed her eyes at Uncle Tom, willing him to take it up from there.

Tom followed his cue. 'That's right – should be worth eight or ten grand, with the possibility of some more work next year.'

But again, Joan was not impressed. 'Seems to me everybody makes money far too easily these days,' she muttered. 'People have forgotten all about doing an honest day's work for an honest day's money.'

Martin couldn't take much more. The atmosphere in the room was stifling him. He poured a gin and tonic and carried it over to Joan, making the supreme effort to look pleasant. 'Here, have a drink before you cut your cake, Joan,' he said, forcing a smile. 'I've got to go out in a minute.'

Joan looked up at him with a knowing, contemptuous smile on her thin lips. 'Oh, so you're off again, are you? Always rushing about, things to do. It's a pity you can't find more of your time to devote to Cathy.'

Martin's mouth compressed into a firm line as the faked smile flickered out like a candle in the wind. His jaw worked nervously as he made a determined effort to keep his mouth shut.

Cathy stepped in to his defence instead. 'That's not fair, Mum. Martin has clients to see. They're important.'

Joan took a sip of her drink. 'Nothing's more important than your wife and child,' she said flatly. She paused for a second, a malicious smile coming over her face. 'Even if he is somebody else's,' she added, almost casually.

There was a sudden, deathly hush. The atmosphere in the room could have been cut with a knife. In the few seconds of shocked silence which followed Joan's outburst, the hiss of indrawn breath was like a rush of wind.

Joan gloated, momentarily, over her little triumph. Then her mouth dropped open in an exaggerated gesture of surprise. 'Oh dear – I'm sorry,' she muttered. 'I thought everyone in the family knew. I mean, it's not a secret or anything, is it?'

Tom stared at her, stone-faced. 'No, Joan, it's not a secret – '

'Well, there you are then!' Joan's pretence of remorse snapped off as quickly as she had adopted it. 'These things have to be aired, don't they? Brought out into the open.'

'Not now, Mum,' Cathy begged, but her plea fell on deaf ears. Joan was well into her stride now, revelling in being the centre of attention. She turned her attention to Martin.

'I mean, it's not as though you're ashamed of what you've done, Martin. Or at least that's what you keep trying to tell me.' Martin was staring at her with pure, undiluted hate in his eyes. His teeth grated together as he struggled to control his fury. Adopting an aggrieved, puzzled look of innocence, Joan looked up at her daughter. 'What have I said? I don't understand.'

Martin found his voice at last. 'You understand bloody well, you evil old witch,' he hissed. He rose on the balls of his feet, looking as though he was going to throw himself at her. Ian jumped up, rushing across the room to restrain him as Tom moved protectively to his sister's side. Martin struggled impotently against Ian's grip for a moment before his shoulders slumped. He looked over at Cathy with desperation in his eyes, anguish contorting his features. 'God help me Cathy, but I'll kill the old bitch. I swear it.'

Shrugging himself free, Martin turned away and stormed out of the room as Cathy burst into uncontrollable tears.

Cathy was still crying as she turned off the road and drove up the long gravel drive of the Millar Fertility Clinic. She seemed to have done little else for the last ten hours. For the first time in their married life, Martin had not returned home after storming out of the house the previous night, although this in itself was not a major source of worry. Cathy trusted him, and was secure enough to know that there was not, and never had been, anyone else. Martin had probably got well and truly drunk, checked into an hotel for the night, and would be home when he managed to pull himself together again.

What had upset her more than anything else was not having anyone to talk to. Finally, after spending half the morning just moping around the house and trying to avoid her mother, she had thought of Dr Millar. She still wasn't sure what she could actually say to him, or what he could possibly do about it, but she had come anyway.

She stopped the car outside the large, detached house and climbed out. Heaving herself up the four concrete steps, she rang the bell underneath the discreet little brass plate built into the wall.

The door was opened by Dr Millar himself. After a brief show of surprise, he regarded Cathy's tear-stained face with genuine concern. 'Whatever's the matter Cathy? This is the time when you should be at your happiest.'

Millar's wife, Ruth, appeared in the reception hall behind him. She was slightly younger than her husband, somewhere in that indeterminate period between forty and forty-five, and invariably hugged him like a shadow. Seeing Cathy's wretched state, she chided him gently, like a mother hen. 'What are you thinking of, Colin – keeping the poor girl standing on the step like that? Can't you see how upset she is?'

Ruth pushed past him, taking Cathy's arm in a gentle but insistent grip. 'Come on in, Cathy. I'll make you a nice cup of tea and you can tell us all about it.'

Cathy was suddenly glad she had come. The Millars were nice people, caring people. In fact, it was this warmth and personal attention which had helped her to make the decision to have the A.I.D. just as much as Dr Millar's medical qualifications. Feeling better already, Cathy allowed Ruth Millar to lead her through into the couple's private drawing-room.

Ruth helped Cathy to lower herself gently into a low, comfortable sofa. 'I'll go and make that tea,' she murmured, excusing herself as Colin Millar seated himself in an easy chair opposite and regarded Cathy with a professional, yet compassionate, expression.

'Now, suppose you tell me what this is all about,' he said gently.

Cathy smiled at him nervously, feeling slightly guilty about off-loading her personal and family troubles on the man. 'Look, Dr Millar – I'm sorry to just turn up on your doorstep like this,' she murmured apologetically. 'But the truth is, I just couldn't think of anyone else to turn to.'

Millar dismissed the apology with a faint shake of his head. 'Nonsense, Cathy – you don't have to apologise. I told you right from the start that we would both be here for you if you needed us for counselling right through your pregnancy.' He paused, a slightly impish grin crossing his face. 'You might think of it as after-sales service,' he went on, 'although I prefer to use the term "on-going support".'

Cathy was starting to relax now, drawing comfort from Millar's gentle, almost paternal, concern. Taking a deep breath, she began to confide in him, sparing no details as she recounted the events which had led up to Martin rushing out of the house.

Ruth Millar returned with a tray of tea and biscuits before she had finished. Placing the tray down on a coffee-table, she sat herself next to Cathy and listened patiently to the rest of the story.

'I just don't understand why my mother is the way she is,' Cathy concluded, eventually. 'I know she's very bitter because our father left her when we were very young – but then why does she seem to resent my marriage so much?'

Ruth placed her hand very lightly on Cathy's knee, squeezing it gently. 'Perhaps inviting her in the first place was a mistake, Cathy.'

Cathy nodded. 'I wanted her to be here for the baby's birth,' she explained. 'I thought it would make her happy, you see.'

Dr Millar leaned forward in his chair. 'It's not your mother's happiness you should be thinking about right now,' he pointed out. 'The vitally important thing is that you put Martin and the baby first.'

Cathy regarded him miserably, reading between the lines. 'You think I should send her home?'

Millar shrugged. 'That has to be your decision, Cathy. It may be a difficult choice to make – but you have to make it.'

Cathy was silent for a while, considering it all and searching for a compromise. 'Perhaps if you could talk to her?' she suggested, hopefully. 'Help her to see that it's not . . . unnatural.'

Millar and his wife exchanged a brief, slightly dubious glance. There was another thoughtful silence. Finally, Ruth Millar brightened. 'Look, I have an idea,' she announced. 'Why don't you bring your mother along to the Gibsons' christening tomorrow? We'll be there, and she can see their baby and hold it. A baby says more than a thousand words from a doctor.'

It seemed a wonderful idea, and Cathy seized upon it gratefully, unaware that she was setting in place a sequence of events which would inevitably lead to tragedy.

Chapter Five

It would have been difficult to imagine a more perfect day for a christening. The sun shone brightly, a gentle westerly breeze wafted the smell of summer flowers from neighbouring gardens across the small churchyard, and the women in their bright dresses and colourful hats lent an air of festivity to the idyllic scene.

Cathy parked the car across the road from the church and got out, opening the passenger door for her mother, noting the resigned, miserable look on her face. 'Look, Mum – try to relax and enjoy yourself, will you?' Cathy urged. 'And try to be nice to Rob and Michelle Gibson – they're friends of ours. Oh yes, and they're calling their baby Scott, by the way.'

Joan Mathieson sniffed haughtily. 'I give as I get,'

she muttered. 'But I'll take no truck with these high-falutin types with their airs and graces.'

Cathy smiled at her mother indulgently. 'They're hardly that,' she pointed out. 'Rob's a policeman and Michelle used to work in the local grocery store. You'll like them, I promise.'

Unconvinced, Joan followed her daughter across the road towards the crowded churchyard. Cathy's eyes scanned the throng of people, searching for a friendly face. Not surprisingly, Rob and Michelle Gibson were the centre of attention, hemmed in by a tight knot of relatives and friends all admiring the baby. It was not a good time to disturb them, Cathy realised. Looking around again, she noticed Ruth Millar, standing on her own close to the church doors.

Taking her mother's arm, Cathy led her over. 'Mum, this is Mrs Millar, Dr Millar's wife. She helps him run the clinic.'

Ruth held out her hand in greeting, smiling warmly. 'Pleased to meet you,' she said to Joan.

The proffered hand was not accepted. Joan merely grunted, nodding her head curtly and eyeing Ruth Millar with undisguised suspicion. Cathy flashed the woman a brief look of apology and led her mother away again. As they turned, the Revd Ken Morton came out of the church to stand on the threshold, gazing up at the blue sky with a look of satisfaction on his face.

It was a heaven-sent opportunity, Cathy thought. Even her mother would not dare to openly snub a man of the cloth. She tapped Revd Morton on the sleeve, getting his attention. 'Reverend Morton – this is my mother. She's staying with us until the baby is born.'

Morton held out his hand, which Joan took, albeit grudgingly. 'Nice to meet you,' he murmured politely.

He smiled at Joan, but the look of sullen hostility lurking in her eyes made him feel instantly ill at ease. Muttering his excuses, he moved off abruptly into the crowd to greet some of his more regular parishioners.

The loud tolling of the church bells ceased suddenly, ushering the congregation into the church for the start of the service. In the silence which followed, the loudest sounds were those of babies crying. People began to move towards the church doors, breaking up into singles and pairs. Joan turned as if to walk into the church, but Cathy restrained her gently. She held her ground as Rob and Michelle came towards them, at last free of their little entourage. She greeted Michelle with a warm smile. 'Hello, Michelle. A beautiful day for it, don't you think?'

Michelle Gibson nodded happily. She looked quite radiant, and so proud of the baby she cradled in her arms, Cathy thought. She gazed fondly down at the infant, her hand straying absently down to stroke her own distended belly as she did so. Michelle noticed the gesture, and smiled. 'Not long now, Cathy,' she murmured understandingly. 'It'll be your turn soon.'

'Oh, by the way – this is my Mum,' Cathy said, suddenly remembering the main point of the morning. She glanced down at the baby again. 'Do you think Mum could hold him for a moment? She just loves babies.'

'Sure.' Michelle held the child out like a sacrificial offering.

Caught on the hop, Joan had no choice but to take the baby into her own arms, cradling it with well-practised efficiency. The child stirred, letting out a tiny gurgle which could have been a prelude to crying. Instinctively, Joan began to rock it gently, reassuringly.

'Don't you think he has Rob's eyes?' Cathy asked Michelle.

The girl grinned. 'We can't see it,' she admitted. 'Although I can see plenty of *me* in him.'

'What do you think, Mum?' Cathy asked, eager to get her mother involved.

Joan Mathieson stared intently at the baby's features. Suddenly, inexplicably, she gave a little shudder, a strange, faraway expression on her face. She glanced up at Rob, studying his eyes closely for a few seconds before looking away uncomfortably. Then, without a word, she abruptly thrust the child back into Michelle's arms and turned away, hurrying through the church door.

Michelle looked puzzled, even slightly shocked. 'What's wrong with her?' she asked Cathy.

Cathy sighed heavily, shaking her head in exasperation. 'I just don't think I can take much more of this,' she muttered heavily. Forcing an apologetic smile for Michelle and Rob's benefit, she followed her mother into the church.

The peacock butterfly was just a tiny splash of colour almost lost against the more garish splendour of the stained-glass window. It settled against the glass, high above the heads of the congregation, opening and closing its wings slowly and basking in the warmth of the sunlight.

Cathy squeezed herself into the pew beside her mother, who was staring blankly towards the front of the church with that same distant, bemused expression on her face. There was still a considerable amount of settling down as the service started. There were two christenings before Michelle and Rob Gibson's, and there were still guests and family members arriving to take their places. Cathy noticed Dr Millar coming in late, hurrying down the right-hand aisle to slip in beside his wife on the end of the row.

Revd Morton was intoning the words of the opening service. '. . . Go forth, therefore, and make all nations my disciples. Baptise men everywhere – in the name of the Father, the Son, and the Holy Spirit . . .'

The peacock butterfly dropped away from the stained-glass window, fluttering gently downwards. It rested briefly on the bare wooden floor then rose into the air again, seeking the bright shaft of light which beamed into the congregation from the window above. Flashing into the bright light, it glided downwards, finally settling again on the sun-warmed polished wood of the pew in front of Cathy and her mother.

Joan Mathieson had caught the faint, fluttering movements of the butterfly out of the corner of her eye. She turned her head nervously, staring at the insect in horrified fascination. It was still for a moment, its brightly coloured wings closed together as its delicate proboscis gently tested the smell of the rich beeswax polish which adorned the wood of the pews.

Joan tried to look away, returning her attention to the service. But the morbid fascination was too great. Increasingly uncomfortable, Joan turned to stare at it again just as the butterfly flexed its wings and rose into the air once more, performing a little circular, fluttering dance as though trying to choose a direction. Joan's hypnotised eyes followed the creature as it swooped towards Ruth Millar's head, then spiralled up again, wheeled round and began to fly along the pew towards her.

Cathy started with surprise as her mother suddenly

jumped to her feet, clawing feverishly at the back of the pew in front as she struggled to push her way past her pregnant daughter. Joan's face was ashen, her eyes filled with fear. 'Mum – what is it?' Cathy hissed, but her mother was virtually hysterical. Finally managing to ease herself past the bulge of her daughter's stomach, she threw herself out into the aisle before running out of the church as though she was pursued by demons.

The christening service came to an abrupt standstill as Revd Morton was stunned into silence and all heads turned in Cathy's direction. Feeling totally embarrassed, she eased herself out of her seat and made her way laboriously up the aisle after her mother.

Joan Mathieson had run into the small cemetery adjoining the church, where she leaned against a high gravestone, her hand pressed against her mouth as though she was about to vomit. Cathy came up behind her, slipping her arm around her mother's shoulders. 'Mum – what is it?' she questioned again. 'What's wrong?'

Joan's entire body was shuddering. She pulled away violently from Cathy's embrace, half-turning to stare at her daughter through wild, panic-stricken eyes. 'Just leave me alone,' she grated out through her teeth. 'Just go away and leave me alone.'

Shocked and bewildered, Cathy could only take a step back and watch her distraught mother as she appeared to break down completely.

Chapter Six

Joan Mathieson could have been in a catatonic trance. She sat rigid and unmoving in her chair, her head bowed over and her eyes blank and unfocused. Only the flexing of her fingers and the steady clicking of her steel knitting needles gave any sign that she was conscious.

Cathy looked over at her mother with a tired, resigned expression in her eyes. There was nothing more she could do, and frustration was eating away at her inside. Her mother had been like this for three hours now, ever since Cathy had managed to get her home. No explanation for her strange behaviour, no attempt at conversation . . . nothing. She had simply sat herself down, taken out her needles and wool and begun knitting obsessively.

Cathy gathered up her purse and shopping basket.

'Look, I'm just going out to do some shopping,' she called over to Joan, making one last attempt at communication. 'Then I'm meeting Michelle later, in the tea shop. You can come with us if you'd like.' Joan did not look up. Still silent, she merely shook her head and carried on with her knitting. Cathy's frustration finally exploded. 'Oh, please yourself then,' she said irritably, turning towards the door.

Joan spoke for the first time. 'I may not be here when you get back,' she announced, without looking up from her knitting.

Cathy stopped in her tracks, turning to confront her mother. She regarded her silently for some considerable time, finally sighing deeply and heavily. 'Well, that's your choice,' she said flatly. She paused again, a confused mixture of pity and regret on her face. 'Look, I've tried, Mum, I've really tried. I just don't see what else I can do to help you. Perhaps you need to see a doctor.'

Joan Mathieson stopped clicking her needles, and lay her knitting down in her lap. She looked up at her daughter, that dreamy, faraway look in her eyes. 'Your grandmother used to believe that babies who died without being baptised turned into little butterflies,' she murmured, strangely.

Cathy stared at her without comprehension. 'You both had weird ideas,' she observed.

A flicker of a smile crossed her mother's lips. 'We were both midwives,' she said. 'We brought enough of them into the world.' She picked up her knitting again, and returned to it with the same obsessive energy. Cathy listened to the renewed clack of needles for a few more seconds then turned away, shaking her head sadly. There really wasn't anything else she could do or say. She walked out of the room, leaving her mother firmly locked in her own, strange, private little world.

Michelle Gibson peeped round the nursery door to where baby Scott lay silently in his cot. She smiled a trifle ruefully, pleased that the child was sleeping soundly but disappointed that there was no excuse to pick him up for yet another cuddle. It was a dilemma which had faced millions of mothers before her, and would continue to bother millions more. In fact, it took a great effort of will not to at least walk into the room and tuck the sleeping baby in again. Michelle hesitated at the door, torn by the temptation to do so. Finally, she resisted, reminding herself that the baby needed his rest after all the excitement and fuss of the christening. With a last fond glance towards the cot, Michelle ducked out of the room, closing the door quietly behind her.

It was a decision which she would later regret bitterly. For had she checked the sleeping child, she might have noticed the small but quickly spreading dark red patch which was beginning to soak into the bedding. Even as Michelle closed the nursery door, the first drips of fresh, bright blood were starting to drop through the slatted bottom of the cot to form a glistening puddle on the polished lino below.

A shadow fell across the sunny interior of the conservatory as a stealthy figure approached it from the garden outside. A small flotilla of brightly coloured butterflies rose into the air in a fluttering, shimmering cloud, disturbed from their feeding by the unexpected sound of shattering glass.

Joan Mathieson heard nothing, the sound in the background drowned out by the steady clacking of her knitting needles and her total concentration devoted to following the pattern that she knew by heart. The little infant's woollen jacket grew, row by row, as Joan poured herself into the task, forcing all other thoughts from her mind. Inside the conservatory, the butterflies continued to wheel furiously in the air as the intruder finally opened the outer door and came in, creeping quietly towards the inner glass doors to the lounge area.

Joan Mathieson clucked her teeth with annoyance as she dropped a stitch. Frowning, she started to unpick the whole row again, but then stopped, her concentration momentarily broken. Perhaps it was time for a spot of tea, she thought. Rising from her chair, she placed the knitting carefully down on the seat and trudged towards the kitchen.

Behind her, a pair of eyes watched every movement. A white-gloved hand descended on to the handle of the inner conservatory door, testing it with firm but gentle pressure. There was no resistance, the door was unlocked. Smiling with satisfaction, the intruder slipped quietly into the lounge as Joan disappeared through the kitchen doorway. The intruder paused beside the chair where Joan had been sitting, staring at the discarded knitting and the two gleaming, sharply pointed steel needles. It was an open invitation. Slowly, carefully, the white-gloved hand reached down and pulled one of the needles out of the woollen loops. Grasping it purposefully, the intruder moved again, padding softly across the deep-pile carpet in the direction of the kitchen. It was all going to be even easier than expected.

*

Michelle Gibson glanced at her watch. It was nearly three o'clock, she noted. Scott would be waking soon and crying for his afternoon feed, she realised, feeling a warm glow of anticipation at the thought of holding him to her breast again. She was glad that she had maintained her insistence on natural feeding, despite subtle pressures from both Rob and several of her friends. It might be considered somewhat old-fashioned, even faintly quirky – but the sheer intimacy of the act created an even closer bond between mother and child, besides giving her exquisite pleasure. And, in Scott's case, it somehow seemed to go part way to redressing the balance, as it were.

Michelle headed towards the nursery door, unpicking the top buttons of her dress to save time as she walked. Fifteen minutes to feed Scott, another ten to dress him and she could still keep her shopping appointment with Cathy on time. There was still no sound from inside the room, which was all to the good, she thought. It must surely be better for the baby to be aroused to a soft, warm breast and instant gratification than to wake in the sensations of hunger, loneliness and a sense of panic. She reached the nursery door and opened it, tiptoeing across to the cot.

It was the smell which first alerted her, erasing the smile from her face. The sweet, cloying smell of fresh blood. Then her eyes took in the scarlet-stained bedding, the small dark puddle beneath the cot.

Michelle Gibson began to scream as the full horror finally registered.

Joan Mathieson did not scream. There was no time. Alerted by the sound of footsteps behind her, she was only capable of a sudden and muted gasp of indrawn breath as she turned and recognised her attacker. Then the steel knitting needle plunged into her throat. With no more than a choked, gagging sob, Joan's frail body collapsed on to the kitchen floor, dragging the saucepan of boiling eggs with her.

Chapter Seven

Jardine was on the phone as Rob Gibson strolled through the main office, still dressed in his best suit. Seeing him through his open door, Taggart came bounding out of his private office. 'And where were you this morning?' he demanded gruffly.

Gibson looked at him uncertainly, surprised by the question. 'Being a father, sir.'

Taggart glowered at him. 'Not in police time,' he grumbled.

Gibson looked confused. 'But sir, I arranged it with you weeks ago,' he reminded his superior. 'I had time off – for the christening.'

Taggart remembered suddenly. His mind had been occupied with his own christening problems. He smiled at the young DC apologetically. 'Oh, yes. Sorry, I forgot.' He backed away sheepishly.

Jardine came off the phone. He called across to Taggart. 'Seems we've got a murder, sir. A Mrs Joan Mathieson at 25 Fairtree Avenue. It's got all the hallmarks of a domestic.'

Taggart frowned. Domestic murders were invariably tedious and time-consuming. 'You handle it,' he told Jardine. 'I've got other things on my mind – like buying a christening present for my first godson.'

Jardine grinned at him. 'Being a godfather, sir – in police time?'

Taggart shot him a scathing glance. 'Promotion's made you cocky, Michael.' He turned his attention to Jackie Reid. 'Seriously, any suggestions for a suitable present?'

The telephone on her desk rang before she could answer him. She picked it up, then called across to Rob Gibson. 'Rob – it's for you.' She directed her attention back to Taggart, looking thoughtful. 'Well, let's see,' she mused aloud. 'What could you possibly buy for someone called Xavier Livingstone? A do-it-yourself book on how to change your name by deed poll, perhaps?'

'A hundred and one tips on playground fighting?' Jardine put in, adding his own contribution.

The light-hearted banter was cut off abruptly by a strangled sob from Rob Gibson. He dropped the receiver back into its cradle, turning away from Jackie's desk with a shudder. His face was ashen. He looked shaken to the core.

'Rob, whatever is it?' Jackie Reid asked in concern.

Gibson chewed at his lower lip, his body trembling. 'It's my kid,' he blurted out, a catch in his voice. 'He's been rushed into hospital.'

Taggart's reaction was immediate. He jabbed his thumb towards the door. 'Go,' he barked, simply.

Jardine was fishing in his pocket for his car keys. He nodded across the room, first at Jackie Reid and then at Gibson. 'Come on, we'll drive you,' he snapped. He glanced briefly at Taggart, offering an explanation even though one was not necessary. 'The hospital's on the way to Fairtree Avenue.'

Taggart rolled his eyes. 'I don't care if it's on the way to China – just get going.'

Jardine, Reid and Gibson left the office at the run.

Joan Mathieson's body lay face-up in the conservatory. In death, her eyes stared serenely up at the cloud of dancing butterflies which would have terrified her in life. The brightly-coloured insects swarmed over her face and neck, drawn by the irresistible red food despite the presence of Dr Andrews, Jardine and several uniformed police officers.

Andrews dropped to one knee beside the body, staring at Joan Mathieson's throat in fascination. 'Remarkable, truly remarkable,' he muttered under his breath, more for his own benefit than for anyone else's.

'Care to share it with me?' Jardine asked, a trifle irritably.

Dr Andrews did not take his eyes away from the magnificent butterfly which was feeding from the wound in the woman's neck. 'A Malaysian Saturn,' he muttered, without looking up. 'Never thought I'd ever get to actually see one close up. I've got a picture of one at home, on a stamp.'

Jardine sniffed dismissively. 'I'm sure Taggart will be absolutely fascinated to hear that,' he observed with heavy sarcasm. 'But if the wildlife lecture is over, how about some boring details about the corpse? Cause of death, for instance? Murder weapon?'

Andrews managed to tear his eyes away from the butterfly. He glanced up at Jardine, looking slightly guilty. 'Sorry, got a bit carried away there.' He paused for a moment, framing his thoughts. 'From the murderer's point of view, it was either a lucky wound or he had a basic knowledge of human anatomy. An incision directly into the jugular vein, causing immediate and rapid loss of blood. In a victim as old and frail as this, death would have been quite fast. She may even have died immediately from shock.' Andrews paused again. 'As for a murder weapon, look for something long, thin, sharp and probably smooth-edged.'

Jackie Reid had just come in from the lounge in time to catch the end of the conversation. 'How about a steel knitting needle?' she asked.

Andrews nodded. 'That would fit the bill rather nicely.'

Jardine looked at her. 'Found it?' he queried hopefully.

Jackie shook her head. 'Probably just its twin brother. There's one in the lounge which has still got knitting on it, but the other one is missing.'

Dr Andrews was examining the underside of Joan Mathieson's body. 'Judging from the way the victim's clothing is rucked up, I'd say she was killed somewhere else in the house and dragged in here afterwards.'

Jackie Reid beamed at Jardine in triumph. 'Now *there* I can help you out,' she announced. She gestured to Jardine to follow her, leading the way towards the kitchen. She pressed the pedal of a litter bin, flipping up the lid and exposing the contents. It was not a pretty sight. Jardine regarded the messy mixture of blood, egg yolk and screwed-up kitchen towels with an expression of distaste on his face. 'Whoever did it took the time and trouble to clean up the kitchen afterwards,' Jackie observed, nodding her head down at the spotless floor. 'It would seem we have a tidy-minded killer on our hands.'

'Or perhaps a house-proud one?' Jardine suggested, flashing her a querulous glance. He was still backing his original hunch that it was a purely domestic murder. Nothing he had seen so far had suggested anything different, and in fact had reinforced that belief. Certainly the choice of weapon from inside the house pointed to a sudden, opportunist attack rather than a premeditated killing. People who set out to commit murders invariably carried their own weapons.

Jardine called a young uniformed constable over. 'What do we know about the family so far?' he asked.

The constable consulted his notes. 'Not a great deal at the moment, sir,' he admitted. 'The couple who own the house are Martin and Cathy Adams. He's an architect and she doesn't work. The victim is the wife's mother.'

'Has anybody contacted either of them yet?' Jardine wanted to know.

The constable shook his head. 'We telephoned the husband's office,' he informed Jardine. 'He's out on a site visit and can't be contacted. Whereabouts of the wife unknown, but both cars are missing from the garage.'

Jardine assimilated the information, dismissing the young copper with a faint nod. He turned back to Jackie Reid. 'So we wait until one of them comes home,' he said flatly. 'Meanwhile, I'm going to talk to whoever found the body.' He walked outside, grateful to get some fresh air. In the front garden there was only one civilian inside the police cordon. Jardine approached him directly. 'I assume it was you who discovered the body?'

Revd Morton nodded, his face grim. 'Ken Morton,' he said, introducing himself. 'I'm the minister of North Church.'

'Can I ask you what you were doing around the back of the house?' Jardine enquired politely.

'Of course.' Morton took a breath before launching into a calm and businesslike statement of the facts. 'Cathy, her daughter, is in my congregation. Her mother was taken ill in church earlier today and I just came round to see how she was.'

'But why the back of the house?' Jardine asked, slightly puzzled.

Morton's eyes widened slightly, as though he couldn't quite understand the question. 'There was no answer at the front. It seemed the logical thing to do.' He paused for a second, noting the slightly suspicious look in Jardine's eyes. 'I knew about the conservatory, you see,' he added, realising that some further explanation was required. 'I've been here several times before to see her husband's butterflies. I noticed the broken pane, looked in – and saw Mrs Mathieson lying on the floor. That's when I called the police.'

It all seemed fairly straightforward, Jardine thought. There was probably nothing more to be gained from that particular line of enquiry for the moment. He changed his tack. 'When you say she was taken ill, what do you mean, exactly?'

'She just jumped up and ran out of the church, in the middle of a christening service,' Morton explained. 'As though she was going to be sick. Cathy told me later that her mother had a phobia about butterflies – and it seemed there was one fluttering around inside the church at the time.' He broke off, a slightly bemused expression coming over his face. 'Some people are afraid of the strangest things.'

Jardine had to agree with him. However, it was a point worth following through. 'You mean a real pathological phobia?' he stressed.

Morton nodded. 'Apparently. Perhaps it was something which happened to her when she was a child,' he suggested.

Jardine smiled thinly to himself. Another amateur psychologist, he thought. But there was just one little thing which didn't ring quite true. His eyes narrowed slightly as he confronted Morton directly again. 'So, knowing that Mrs Mathieson had an irrational fear of butterflies – you went round to look for her in a conservatory you knew to be full of them?' he asked.

Revd Morton stared at him in silence. He didn't have an answer for that one.

Chapter Eight

Rob and Michelle Gibson both jumped to their feet from their seat in the waiting-room as the casualty ward doors swung open. Perhaps their agonising wait was over at last. Rob hugged his wife tightly to his side, his eyes fixed intently on the expression of the young doctor who came out through the doors, searching the man's face for the slightest sign of a clue.

The doctor was smiling. Rob's heart jumped, hope surging within him again after the terrible, morbid terror which had gripped him for the past two hours. 'Your baby's going to be fine,' the doctor announced. 'He's perfectly stable now, and we don't see any potential problems.'

Michelle let out a choked little sob. Rob felt his wife go limp in his arms. He lowered her gently back on to the seat. Relief rose up from his stomach like a solid knot, lodging in his throat. 'Thank God,' he managed to croak out. He stared silently at the doctor, fighting to stop himself from breaking into tears. Finally managing to regain control of himself, he asked, 'What was the matter with him?'

The doctor adopted a look of professional reassurance. 'He had what we call an intersusseption. That's an intestinal blockage which can produce a haemorrhage. Luckily, your wife noticed it in time, before he lost too much blood. But he's fine now, and we'll be giving him a blood transfusion. There's nothing to worry about, I assure you.'

The wonderful, unbelievable news had finally sunk into Michelle's consciousness. She looked up at the doctor, her face calm and composed. 'Do you need either of us for a donor, doctor?' she volunteered. 'We both give blood regularly, so we're used to it.'

The doctor smiled at her gently. 'The last thing either of you need right now is any more stress,' he pointed out. 'You've both been through a pretty unpleasant experience. Besides, we happen to have quite good stocks of Type B blood at the moment.'

Under the circumstances, and to an average parent, the doctor's words might well have gone unnoticed. But Rob Gibson was a policeman, trained to listen carefully to statements and be on the look-out for anomalies. He picked up on the last few words at once, reacting instinctively. 'Sorry, doctor, but you must have made a mistake,' he said firmly. 'Scott has to be blood group O, like Michelle and myself. As my wife said, we're both regular blood donors, so we know these things.'

The doctor's face clouded over. He looked a little unsure of himself. 'I assure you there's no mistake, Mr

Gibson,' he announced, almost defensively. 'We always check these things carefully – even more so in the case of an infant, as you might expect. Your child's blood group is definitely Type B.'

'But how can that possibly be?' Michelle asked, a nervous catch in her voice.

The doctor's eyes flickered over her face, then turned away, as though he were unwilling, or unable, to sustain eye-to-eye contact with her. He now looked openly unsure of his ground, even embarrassed. 'I'm sorry,' he muttered awkwardly. 'There's no doubt.'

There was a long, pregnant silence. Finally Rob spoke in a very deliberate, very calm voice. 'Doctor, would you mind leaving us alone for just a minute?' he asked.

The medic seemed to take the request as a personal reprieve. He grasped at it a trifle over-eagerly. 'Of course.' He turned, starting to walk away, then paused, looking back at Michelle uncertainly. 'Look – if you need to talk to me again, I'll be in my office.' He hurried off back through the swing doors, clearly relieved to escape the strained, tense atmosphere in the waiting-room.

Michelle's eyes were shocked and confused as she looked up at her husband. 'Rob – what's going on?' she asked nervously.

She met only the cold, accusing stare of a man shaken to his very core. A man who has just had the very essence of his being, his manhood, stripped away from him. 'I don't know. Supposing you tell me.'

Michelle racked her brains for an answer, finally coming up with the only wild possibility which made any kind of sense at all. Unthinkable and frightening as it was, Michelle had to voice it. 'They must have made some sort of mistake at the clinic,' she said, her voice trembling.

'How?' Rob demanded, the same cold look in his eyes. The pain inside him was like a razor-sharp icicle being turned, slowly, in his gut.

Michelle shook her head distractedly. 'I don't know ... I just don't understand any of this,' she sobbed, on the verge of tears again. She stared at her husband's face intently, seeing the anger and accusation behind the pain. Realisation struck her with almost physical force, catapulting her over the edge of confusion into blind panic. Her hands clawed at the material of her husband's jacket, as though fighting to keep hold of him, knowing that he was slipping away from her. Her choked, desperate voice teetered on the verge of hysteria. 'Oh my God, Rob ... you can't think ...'

Rob's eyes were filling with tears. 'I don't know what I'm thinking,' he muttered, wretchedly.

Michelle pulled him towards her, against his resistance. She buried her face in his stomach, sobbing uncontrollably. 'I swear, Rob,' she managed to gasp, 'I swear on Scott's life there was never anybody else. You've got to believe that.'

It was all too much to bear, to cope with. Knowing that Michelle needed him so much, aching to be able to offer her some comfort, Rob could only stand there like a statue, frozen inside the cocoon of his own anguish.

The initial shock was beginning to pass now, leaving only the emptiness and the sense of guilt.

Cathy Adams sat in Taggart's private office, sipping at the cup of tea which Jackie Reid had made for her. She looked across the desk at Taggart, who had hardly said a word since Jackie had brought her in to the station. Experience had taught him that a gentle approach worked best in these cases, and it didn't take a PhD to realise that Cathy was only days away from delivering her baby. So he'd given her time to volunteer whatever information she might be willing to give, rather than subject her to direct questioning.

'I should have stayed with her,' Cathy murmured, miserably. 'I should have tried to be more patient with her, made more of an effort.'

Taggart regarded her with an unusually benign, reassuring expression. 'It's not unusual for a relative of a murder victim to feel a sense of guilt,' he pointed out gently. 'But there's no reason for it. You have nothing to blame yourself for.'

Cathy seemed to take some comfort from the words. She sipped at her tea again. 'She said . . . she said she might not be there when I got back,' Cathy went on hesitantly.

'What do you think she meant by that?' Jackie Reid wanted to know.

Cathy shrugged hopelessly. 'I don't know – I suppose she meant that she might have gone home.'

Taggart took it up, probing delicately. 'Why would your mother want to go home, Cathy? Wasn't she happy staying with you? What sort of a state of mind was she in when you left her?'

Cathy shook her head. 'She didn't feel comfortable in the house – I know that,' she volunteered. 'And I think she was worried about what might happen when Martin came home. Then there was the business with the butterfly in the church this morning.'

'Martin? That's your husband, is it?' Taggart asked.

Cathy nodded. 'They didn't get on very well.' She

paused, realising that she had said more than she meant to. It suddenly seemed very important to qualify the statement, protect her husband in his absence. 'It wasn't really Martin's fault,' she added, defensively. 'He really did make an effort to be nice to her, but it was difficult for him. Mum always had such narrow, old-fashioned ideas, you see.'

Taggart nodded understandingly, sensing that he might be on to something. He flashed a discreet glance in Jackie Reid's direction, giving her the go-ahead to take it up, playing the woman's angle.

'Mothers can be difficult,' she said, looking suitably sympathetic. 'Was there anything in particular that your mother and Martin didn't see eye to eye about?'

Cathy nodded, responding to Jackie's apparent concern. 'They fell out about the baby,' she said. 'She just couldn't seem to accept the idea.'

Jackie looked a little puzzled. 'That you and your husband were having a child?'

The faintest trace of a smile passed across Cathy's face. 'That it was quite normal,' she corrected. 'You see, the baby isn't really Martin's. We tried for a couple of years, and finally went to a special clinic. It turned out that Martin had a problem, so we decided to go for artificial insemination by donor.' Cathy paused for a moment. 'The trouble was, Mum thought it was unnatural.'

'And how did Martin take that?' Taggart wanted to know.

Cathy was guarded. 'He was upset, of course. We'd talked it over for months, and we were both very happy about it. We *are* happy about it,' she added, emphasising the point.

'Upset?' Jackie put in. 'How upset? What did your mother say to him?'

Cathy's face reflected her inner turmoil. She had talked herself into a trap in which she seemed to be betraying her husband in some way. Yet her mother's death was a stark and unpalatable fact, and she needed to get to the truth about it. 'She called him half a man,' Cathy said honestly. 'She kept rubbing it in that I was carrying another man's baby inside me.'

Jackie raised her eyes in Taggart's direction. The expression on his face said just about everything there was to say. Men had murdered before, on much less provocation.

'When did you last see your husband, Cathy?' Taggart asked.

Cathy looked evasive, aware that she was unwittingly making things look blacker and blacker for Martin without meaning to. But, short of a direct lie, she couldn't see what else she could do. 'Last night,' she admitted finally. 'He left the house to see a client and didn't come back – but that's not unusual.'

Taggart was sceptical. 'Your husband storms out and doesn't come home – and you say it isn't unusual?' he queried.

Cathy was becoming increasingly uncomfortable. She needed to make Taggart see the truth, understand. 'It's not what you think,' she said, her voice almost pleading. 'Martin walked out because he didn't want to get into a row in front of relatives. We had my brother and uncle over, you see – for Mum's birthday. And anyway, as I told you – he had a client to see. They probably had a few drinks together, and Martin wasn't in a fit state to drive home. He'll have checked into a hotel – he's done it before.'

Taggart decided to let it go for the moment. He already had a pretty good idea of his line of questioning when Martin Adams did eventually show up. He left it to Jackie Reid to clear up the last few loose ends.

'Who did you go shopping with?' Jackie wanted to know.

'I was going to meet a friend in town, but she didn't show up,' Cathy answered.

'Do you mind telling us her name?'

Cathy shook her head. 'Not at all. It's Michelle Gibson. Her husband Rob is a detective constable here.' Caught unawares, Jackie was unable to control the sudden look of concern which crossed her face. Cathy picked up on it at once. 'What is it? What's wrong?'

'Nothing, Cathy – nothing at all,' Jackie said, recovering herself.

But with a woman's instinct, Cathy knew she was lying.

Chapter Nine

Still seething with anger and confusion, Rob Gibson brought his car to a sudden and fierce halt in the driveway of the Millar Clinic, spraying gravel over the nearby lawn. Jumping out, he slammed the door behind him and bounded up the steps to the front entrance, ringing the bell and pounding on the solid wooden door with his clenched fists.

Ruth Millar answered it, looking understandably worried. She stared at Gibson's angry face in puzzlement. 'Mr Gibson?' Ruth glanced at her watch. 'Look, the clinic is closed now. Dr Millar and I were just going home.'

'Not until I get some sort of an explanation,' Gibson growled at her. Beyond caring about common courtesy, he threw his weight against the door and pushed it fully open, forcing his way past her. He stopped in the entrance hall, turning back to confront her. 'Well, where is he?' he demanded gruffly.

Colin Millar came out of his private office, dressed to leave. He stopped in mid-stride, recognising Gibson with a look of surprise on his face. 'Is there some sort of a problem?'

Gibson strode up to him, jabbing his finger in the man's chest aggressively. 'I'll tell you what the problem is,' he hissed angrily. 'In your office – now!'

Millar stepped back uncertainly under the assault. He turned, moving back to the door of his office and opening it. Gibson practically pushed him into the room. Mystified, and more than a little worried, Ruth followed them in and closed the door behind her.

Millar retreated behind his desk and sank down in a chair. He looked up at Gibson's irate face with narrowed eyes. 'Now, do you mind telling me what all this is about?' he asked.

Gibson took a deep breath, rationalising his thoughts and trying to suppress his anger. He was only partially successful. 'My wife and I came to this clinic because we'd been trying for years to have a baby without success,' he opened.

Millar nodded, cutting in. 'Yes – and we identified the problem,' he muttered calmly. 'And now you have a bouncing little son.'

It was the wrong thing to say. Gibson jumped forward, slamming his bunched fist down on Millar's desktop. 'But I don't, do I?' he thundered.

Millar's eyes flickered with uncertainty. 'Look, Mr Gibson – why don't you take a seat, try to calm yourself and let's discuss this like sensible men?'

Gibson's temper flared up again. 'How the hell can I

be calm?' he demanded. 'I've just found out that I'm not the baby's father.'

Ruth Millar's reaction was immediate. 'That's impossible,' she said flatly.

'He had a haemorrhage because of an intestinal blockage,' Gibson went on. 'He needed a blood transfusion. Only his blood was Group B – and he couldn't possibly have got that from me, or my wife.'

Millar looked defensive. 'There has to be some sort of mistake.'

Gibson glared at him. 'Oh yes, there's been a mistake all right. And that mistake was made right here in this clinic. What I want to know is how, and who's responsible?'

Millar shook his head in confusion. 'I really am at a loss to account for it,' he muttered.

'There's just no way that your semen could become mixed up with that of a donor,' Ruth Millar put in. 'It just couldn't happen.'

'I performed the operation myself,' Millar said, taking it up again. 'It was a straightforward transfer of your semen into your wife because of the hostile mucus at the neck of her womb. You watched me perform the transfer yourself.'

The reminder brought Gibson up with a jolt. Confusion won the battle with his anger once again. 'But it wasn't straightforward, was it? Something went wrong – and I intend to find out what.'

Dr Millar was silent for a while, finally sighing. 'I just don't know what to say to you,' he admitted at last. 'There is no explanation I can give you.'

Gibson chewed at his bottom lip in frustration. 'Then I'll find someone who can,' he muttered heavily. He stared at Millar impotently for a few more moments, finally realising that the man was unable, or unwilling, to give him any answers. Anger had failed. Straight questioning had failed. There remained only the power of threat. Gibson stepped forward, jabbing an outstretched finger in Millar's face. 'Just take my word, you haven't heard the last of this,' he told the man, firmly. 'I'll get to the bottom of this if it's the last thing I do.'

There was nothing more to say. Gibson turned on his heel and strode out of the office, leaving Ruth and Colin Millar to gaze at each other with shocked, worried expressions on their faces.

Chapter Ten

Gibson looked totally shell-shocked as he walked into the main office like a man in a trance. Seeing his pale, shaken features, Jardine moved towards him, a sympathetic expression on his face. 'What are you doing back here?' he asked, concernedly. 'You should be with your wife and child.'

The show of support was appreciated. Rob Gibson forced a brief, thin smile on to his face. 'It's all right,' he assured his colleague. 'Michelle's fine and the baby's out of danger.'

Genuine relief showed on Jardine's face. 'Thank heavens. We were all worried about you,' he murmured. 'What was wrong, anyway?'

Gibson shrugged faintly. 'It was something they called an intersusseption – some kind of intestinal blockage. It caused him to haemorrhage, but apparently it looked a lot more serious than it really was.'

Jardine nodded thoughtfully, frowning slightly. 'But you still shouldn't be here,' he said, mildly reproving. 'I think we can manage to get by without you for one evening.'

'Thanks, Mike.' Gibson's smile was a little longer this time. He sighed. 'Look, Mike – have you got anything on right now? The truth is, I need to talk to someone.'

Jardine shook his head. 'I'm clear at the moment.' He paused for a second, wondering whether or not to tell Gibson that they had just brought in Martin Adams for questioning. The man had probably had enough shocks for one day, he figured. He hesitated for too long, forgetting what an astute young copper Gibson really was, despite his current problems.

'Mike – there's something you're not telling me, isn't there?' Gibson demanded.

Jardine sighed, mildly cursing himself for his oversight. He was thoughtful for a while. 'It's just that Taggart's interviewing a friend of yours right now,' he admitted finally. 'Martin Adams. His mother-in-law was found murdered this morning.' He paused again, flashing Gibson a regretful glance. 'I'm afraid it doesn't look too good for him at the moment. It's got every sign of being a standard domestic.'

Gibson looked stunned. He nodded his head in the direction of Jardine's office. 'Can we talk?'

'Sure.' Jardine ushered Gibson in and closed the door firmly. Perching himself on the edge of his desk, he waited for Rob Gibson to sit himself down then eyed the young DC questioningly. 'You've obviously got something on your mind. What is it?'

Just for the moment, the shock news about his friend had pushed Gibson's personal problems aside. 'How sure are you – about Martin?' he asked Jardine.

Jardine shrugged. 'It looks pretty clear-cut at the moment,' he admitted.

Gibson shook his head doubtfully. 'I don't know,' he muttered. 'I just can't see Martin as a murderer, somehow. What would be his motive?'

Jardine could see no reason to withhold any details from his colleague. He launched into a brief resumé. 'The fact of the matter is that his wife is carrying another man's child. They had it by anonymous donor at a fertility clinic. His mother-in-law had been needling him about not being able to produce children of his own, and apparently called him only half a man. It looks like it all just boiled over.'

Rob Gibson's face seemed to have gone even paler, Jardine thought. 'Rob – are you sure you're all right?' he asked.

Gibson nodded, drawing in a long, deep breath. 'This fertility clinic – run by Dr Colin Millar and his wife, right?'

Jardine reacted with surprise. 'Yes – but how did you know that?'

Gibson was silent and thoughtful for a while. Finally, he looked up at Jardine with a slightly embarrassed expression on his face. 'Look, Mike – can I say something to you in the deepest confidence?'

'Of course,' Jardine answered without even considering it. He was intrigued.

'Michelle and I went to that same clinic,' Gibson blurted out suddenly, as though he was glad to finally share a secret. 'That's where we first met Martin and Cathy Adams, by the way.'

'And?' Jardine prompted gently, sensing that Gibson needed to establish a close confidence.

'Well, anyway – we found out that Michelle had this problem, and we decided to have Scott by artificial insemination,' Gibson went on.

'Donor?'

Gibson shook his head. 'Not by donor – the child was supposed to be mine.' He paused for a moment, struggling to control the sense of outrage which was beginning to boil up from his gut once again. 'But I've just found out that Scott *isn't* mine. They needed blood for a transfusion, and it seems he's got a different blood group.' Jardine looked a little nonplussed. 'It means that I can't be the child's father,' Gibson explained. 'It's a medical impossibility, take my word for it. I know about these things.'

Jardine was stunned into silence for a while. He looked at Gibson awkwardly, not sure what to say, or what the man *expected* him to say. 'Rob, I'm sorry,' he murmured finally. 'But why exactly are you telling me all this?'

Gibson shifted uncomfortably in his chair, knowing that he was on uncertain ground. 'I've just come from the clinic,' he told Jardine. 'Dr Millar didn't seem to want to give me any sort of an explanation.'

Jardine frowned. He still wasn't quite sure what Rob was driving at. 'Maybe he was just as baffled as you are,' he suggested.

Gibson shook his head. 'No – it's more than that, I know it,' he said emphatically. There was a pleading look in his eyes as he regarded Jardine again. 'Look, Mike – I need some answers, and I just don't know where to turn.'

Jardine got the message, finally. He considered the

matter for some time. At last, he faced Gibson directly, trying to look as positive as he could. 'I can't make any promises, you understand?'

Gibson nodded. 'Anything you can do, I'd be grateful. I'm desperate, Mike.'

'I'll do what I can,' Jardine promised him. He stood up, waiting for Gibson to get up from his chair. 'Now you get yourself home to your wife and try to relax,' he told the young DC.

Gibson nodded, smiling at Jardine gratefully. He looked a lot better than when he had come in. 'Thanks,' he said simply. He turned towards Jardine's office door, then stopped on an afterthought. 'Listen, about Martin Adams,' he muttered. 'I've got to know him pretty well over the last year, and I just don't see him as a killer.'

'I'll keep that in mind,' Jardine said quietly.

Jardine opened the door of Interview Room 3 cautiously, slipping quietly into the room where Taggart and Jackie Reid were quizzing Martin Adams. Taggart glanced up briefly, his face registering nothing. Taking this as permission for his continued presence, Jardine closed the door quietly and stayed discreetly in the background.

Taggart turned his attention back to Adams. 'Come on, Martin. We understand how you must have felt. Every word she said was a blow to your pride, a dig at your manhood. There's not many men could take that sort of treatment without blowing up.'

Adams glared at him in stubborn defiance. 'I've told you – I got out of the house because I didn't want to have a full-scale row in front of Cathy. The baby's almost due.'

'But you went back, didn't you?' Taggart suggested. 'You went back to have it out with your mother-in-law – perhaps persuade her to go home. But she started in on you again, and you saw red.'

Adams shook his head. 'It wasn't like that,' he maintained. 'I told you, I got a bit drunk and I stayed in the Balmoral Hotel. You've got the credit card receipt to prove that. I went straight to work in the morning, and I didn't come back to the house until this evening, when your officers picked me up.'

'We think you came back a bit earlier than that,' Jackie put in. 'We think you returned to the house this afternoon, knowing that your wife had arranged to go shopping with a friend and realising that your mother-in-law would be alone. You rowed again, you lost your temper . . . and you killed her.'

Adams faced her squarely, his face impassive. 'I told you – I was working all day. I was miles away.'

'But nobody saw you,' Taggart pointed out. He referred back to some notes he had made earlier. 'You claim to have been at this construction site in Anniesland from just after midday to six o'clock. Yet you spoke to no one, the site foreman doesn't recall seeing you, and you never checked in with your office. That's a long time to stay invisible, Martin.'

Adams shrugged. 'It's a big site. Seventeen industrial complexes and an office block. People were busy.'

'Where did you get your hard hat?' Taggart asked suddenly. Adams regarded him blankly. 'Your hard hat,' Taggart repeated. 'Everyone on a construction site is supposed to wear one, for safety reasons.'

Adams glowered at him. 'I didn't bother,' he muttered.

'That's illegal,' Jackie put in, rather pointedly.

Adams sniffed contemptuously. 'So I broke the law. But I didn't kill anyone.'

'We think you did,' Taggart said flatly. 'We think you waited until you knew your wife was out of the house and you came home. Your mother-in-law was killed just after three o'clock. That gave you plenty of time to do it, clean up and then drag the body into the conservatory where it wouldn't be discovered until later.' He broke off for a while to let this sink in. 'Or was that just a little extra touch of irony, Martin? Putting Joan Mathieson's body in amongst the butterflies you knew she was so terrified of?'

Adams stared at him sullenly. 'That's crazy,' he said. 'Anyway, the conservatory glass had been smashed from the outside, I saw it. Why should I want to break into my own house?'

Taggart dismissed the objection carelessly. 'Perhaps to put us off the track,' he suggested. 'Make us think it was an outside job.'

'What was it she said to you that finally made you lose your rag?' Jackie asked him. 'Did she call you half a man again, Martin? Did she cast aspersions on your virility?'

Adams jumped to his feet suddenly, kicking his chair backwards. He lunged across the desk towards Jackie Reid, glaring at her with blind fury in his eyes. His voice rose in an angry shout. 'Damn you, can't you get it into your head that I didn't kill her?' he screamed.

Jackie Reid didn't even flinch. She regarded Adams with an aloof, almost triumphant expression, as though she had just proved something. 'That's a nasty temper you have there, Martin,' she pointed out in a calm, quiet voice.

Adams gritted his teeth, controlling himself with an

effort. His temper subsiding, he sank back down into his chair and glanced at Taggart. 'For Christ's sake, you're a man,' he appealed to him. 'How would you like it to have someone rubbing it in that you're incapable of fathering a child?'

Taggart regarded him with a slightly mocking smile playing about his lips. 'Exactly our point,' he murmured, tellingly. He rose to his feet. 'Well, that'll be all for the moment, Mr Adams. I'll probably want to talk to you again a bit later.'

'You're holding me?' Adams asked.

Taggart shrugged. 'You're helping us with our enquiries.' He led the way out of the interview room, signalling for a uniformed constable to come and look after Martin Adams.

'I thought he was about to crack then, sir,' Jackie Reid said, when they were safely outside in the corridor.

Taggart grinned at her. 'Another "aspersion" on his virility and I think he'd have cracked you,' he observed. He glanced aside at Jardine. 'Did you want to talk to me about something, Michael?'

Jardine was slightly guarded in Jackie's presence. 'Actually, it's a bit delicate, sir,' he murmured.

'How delicate?' Taggart wanted to know.

'Very,' Jardine emphasised. 'And I'd rather talk off the premises, as it were. I'll buy you a beer.'

Jackie Reid took the hint, noting that she hadn't been invited. 'Men's talk, is it?' She waved her notes in the air. 'Well, I suppose I ought to go off and get on with the womanly job of typing up these notes.' Slightly miffed, she strode off towards her desk.

*

Taggart sipped at his pint of bitter. 'So, what's this "delicate" matter you wanted to talk about?'

Jardine filled him in with his conversation with Rob Gibson. When he had finished, Taggart regarded him thoughtfully. 'And you think this might have something to do with the Adams case?'

Jardine gave a slight shrug of his shoulders. 'I don't know, sir,' he admitted. 'But Rob and Michelle are their friends, and they went to the same clinic. There could be some sort of a tie-up.'

Taggart thought for a moment, finally shaking his head. 'No, this is a simple domestic, no more than that,' he said decisively.

Jardine had no choice but to accept the man's assessment. 'Okay – but Rob is still stuck with his problem,' he pointed out. 'As far as I can see, there's no way that a mix-up could have occurred at the clinic. Rob says he produced the semen and it was injected straight into his wife. The only way a mistake could have been made is . . . if it wasn't a mistake at all, if you see what I mean.'

Taggart looked at him curiously. 'No, Michael, I'm not sure that I do,' he admitted frankly. He took another sip at his beer before looking back at Jardine with a slightly sardonic smile on his face. 'Now, correct me if I haven't got this right, but are you telling me that we ought to be investigating a suspicious *birth*?'

Jardine looked sheepish. 'Something like that, sir.' He eyed Taggart cautiously. 'Look, I know it's a bit out of left field.'

Taggart let out a short laugh. 'Left field?' he muttered sarcastically. 'It's not even on the bloody pitch.'

Jardine looked suitably admonished. 'Well, I just thought there might be something we could do,' he muttered defensively. 'Rob is one of ours.'

Taggart was silent for a long while, thinking about that last remark. Finally, he relented. 'Well, just be discreet about it,' he warned, flashing Jardine a canny wink.

Chapter Eleven

Ruth Millar fidgeted impatiently as her husband adjusted his tie in the hallway mirror for perhaps the sixth time. She checked her watch. It was already fifteen minutes past nine, and the drive to the clinic would take at least another ten. 'Colin, you look fine,' she muttered peevishly. 'Now can we get going? Or have you forgotten that Angus and Fiona McKenzie have an appointment at half-past nine?'

Dr Millar showed no sign of urgency, merely taking a comb out of his inside pocket and starting to tidy his hair. It was almost as if he was stalling for time, Ruth thought. As though he had some reason for putting off going to the clinic for as long as possible. She waited another few seconds as Colin began to adjust his tie yet again before losing her temper. She headed towards the door. 'Either you're coming now or I go without you,' she threatened.

Reluctantly, Millar tore himself away from the mirror. 'I'll just go and get my briefcase,' he announced irritatingly, turning to walk with almost exaggerated slowness up the stairs. Ruth stood there quietly fuming until he returned, at the same snail-like pace.

'We'll take your car, it's faster,' she snapped at him as they eventually stepped out of the front door. She led the way to Colin's brand-new Ford Probe, waiting for him to open the doors.

Climbing in, Millar slipped the key into the ignition, but did not start the car immediately. Instead, he fiddled pointlessly with the rear-view mirror for another few time-consuming seconds. Eventually, as though they had all the time in the world, Millar started the engine, slipped the car into gear and cruised sedately down the front drive into the roadway. Ruth fumed with impatience as they purred down the empty street at less than twenty-five miles an hour.

She glanced sideways, studying her husband's face, wondering if there was something worrying him. He had been unusually quiet all morning, had refused breakfast, and appeared to be strangely preoccupied. Even now, his expression was curiously blank, like someone sleepwalking.

'Colin – is anything wrong?' Ruth asked him. There was no answer. Millar's face remained impassive. 'Is it this business with the Gibsons?' Ruth prompted. 'Is that what's worrying you?'

But again, Millar failed to answer her. He pulled the car to a halt at traffic lights, opposite a junior school. Millar turned his head towards the playground, watching the children enjoy their last few minutes of playtime before morning assembly. The lights turned green, but Millar didn't seem to notice. He continued to stare at the school playground as if fascinated. Behind them, another driver honked his horn impatiently. Millar snapped out of his reverie. With one last glance at the playing children, he slipped the car into gear again and drove on. They completed the journey to the clinic in silence.

Jardine and Jackie Reid were waiting for them on the steps as Millar cruised up the drive. Ruth Millar climbed out of the car, smiling at them both as she assumed them to be potential clients. 'Sorry to be late. Did you want to make an appointment?' she enquired politely.

Realising that she had taken them to be a young married couple, Jardine flushed with embarrassment. Jackie merely looked amused. Hurriedly, Jardine fished in his pocket, producing his ID card. 'Actually, we're police officers,' he explained. 'We'd like to speak to Dr Millar.'

The smile faded from Ruth Millar's face. 'You'll want my husband,' she muttered curtly, nodding towards Colin who was just climbing out of the car. 'Colin – these people are from the police,' she told him, a guarded, questioning look on her face.

Millar regarded them both with a calm, almost resigned, expression. 'Then they'd better come in,' he muttered, stepping past them to the front door of the clinic and unlocking it.

'Are you a doctor too?' Jackie Reid asked Ruth as they stepped into the entrance hall.

Ruth shook her head. 'No, Colin's the doctor and I'm a nursing sister. But we run the clinic together.' She looked into Jackie's eyes, anxiously. 'Look, what's all this about?'

Jackie was polite but businesslike. 'I'm sorry, Mrs Millar, but it's your husband we need to speak to.' She followed Jardine as Millar led the way to his private consulting-room before speaking to the woman again. 'Would you mind leaving us in private, Mrs Millar?'

Ruth bristled with anger. 'Yes, I would,' she complained, vehemently. 'Anything which concerns my husband concerns me as well.'

Jackie flashed an uncertain gaze at Jardine, who could only shrug. They had no powers to exclude Ruth Millar, if she insisted on being involved. They all trooped into Millar's consulting-room as he opened the door.

Millar seated himself behind his desk, looking up at Jardine and Jackie with a poker face. 'Please, have a seat,' he invited. Jardine drew up two chairs. He and Jackie sat down, as Ruth Millar remained standing, posting herself at the side of her husband's desk like some kind of sentinel. There was a strained silence for a while.

Finally, Jardine cleared his throat. 'I expect you know what this is about,' he said, addressing Dr Millar.

Millar nodded, his blank face still not giving anything away. 'Yes, I had guessed.'

Jardine made the formal introductions. 'Dr Millar – I'm Detective Inspector Jardine and this is Detective Constable Reid. We're colleagues of Rob Gibson, who attended this clinic with his wife, Michelle. There appears to be some sort of a problem.' Jardine fell silent, waiting for a response. There was none. Millar continued to stare at him without expression. It was all very odd. Jardine frowned. 'Well?' he prompted, after an awkward pause. 'Do you have any explanation to offer?'

Millar shook his head faintly. 'None at all,' he said simply.

Jardine regarded him with increasing puzzlement. 'You're not even prepared to venture one?' he demanded.

Millar's eyes dropped to his desktop, avoiding Jardine's stare. 'It's a mystery, isn't it?' he murmured in a quiet little voice.

Ruth Millar's face betrayed her own growing sense of confusion and worry. There was something very strange, and very wrong, with her husband's behaviour. 'Look, I'm sure we can come up with a perfectly good explanation, given time,' she put in suddenly. 'Although I can't really see why this has to be a police matter. After all, this has just been thrust upon us, and we're as concerned as the Gibsons.'

Jardine all but ignored her, still focusing his attention on her husband. 'Dr Millar, you must realise that there are ways of finding out who the father is. By DNA fingerprinting, for example.'

Millar seemed to cave in, abruptly. His shoulders slumped. He raised his eyes to meet Jardine's again, a look of total resignation on his face. He drew a deep breath and let out a long, drawn-out sigh. 'That takes some time, as you probably realise. I expect you'd appreciate an answer before then,' he said quietly. He turned towards his wife. 'Ruth, would you leave us alone for a while?'

Ruth's bewildered expression was rapidly changing to one of shocked concern. But the stirrings of angry defiance burned in her eyes. 'You can all throw me out bodily if you like,' she said curtly, standing her ground.

Millar looked up at her, an almost pleading expression on his face. He let out another sigh as he realised she was not going to be budged. He returned his attention to Jardine and Jackie Reid. 'I suppose I always knew that it had to come out some day,' he murmured somewhat distantly. 'But I just didn't expect it to be quite so soon.'

'You knew what would come out?' Jackie Reid asked.

Millar did not look at her, but continued to face Jardine directly. 'I'm the father of Michelle Gibson's baby,' he announced flatly.

Ruth Millar let out a sudden, strangled gasp. Reeling slightly, she backed towards a nearby chair and flopped down weakly, her features frozen in shock. There was a long, completely stunned silence.

Jardine found his voice first. 'Why?' he demanded, in total disbelief.

A wistful little smile flickered across Millar's face. He shrugged his shoulders faintly. 'Why does any man want to be a father?' It was a rhetorical question.

Jardine still couldn't quite bring himself to believe it all. 'You mean you deliberately –'

Millar cut him short. 'Used my own semen? Yes.'

A nasty little suspicion had been festering in Jackie Reid's mind. She voiced it. 'This wasn't the first time – was it?' she demanded.

Millar shook his head. His expression was sad, although there was no obvious sign of shame, even remorse, on his face. 'No, it wasn't the first time,' he muttered, agreeing with her.

'In those cases where artificial insemination was by donor – it must have been very tempting for you,' Jackie went on.

Millar nodded. 'Yes, it was.'

Jackie Reid was silent for a while. Finally, she spoke

again. 'How many children are we talking about, Dr Millar? One . . . two . . . more?'

'About sixty,' Millar responded.

There was another explosive gasp from Ruth Millar. She pushed herself to her feet unsteadily, reeling back against the nearest wall like a drunk. With a trance-like expression on her face, she began to stagger towards the door. Jackie Reid jumped forward to steady her, fearing that the woman was about to collapse in a faint. With surprising strength, Ruth shrugged her off and managed to make it to the door. Opening it, she lurched out of the consulting-room without uttering a word. Jackie closed the door behind her, turning back to Colin Millar. His face was much more animated now, his whole manner more open and relaxed. It was as though his confession had relieved some terrible inner burden. He even smiled at her.

'Ruth can't have children,' he explained, almost chattily. 'Strange that – don't you think? A fertility clinic doctor whose wife is unable to have children?'

'So to make up for it, you impregnated *sixty* women?' Jardine demanded, incredulously.

Millar looked a little aggrieved. 'Not actually that many. Some had twins, you see.' His expression lightened again. He beamed at Jardine, as though he was actually starting to enjoy his confession. 'To tell you the truth, I've wanted to tell someone about this for a long time,' he went on happily. 'The more I did it, the easier it seemed to become, but of course I could never confide in Ruth. It was a strange feeling – I was proud of my children, but I couldn't tell anyone about them.'

It was Jackie Reid's turn to be totally incredulous. 'Proud?' she queried. 'You're actually *proud* of what you've done?'

Millar smiled at her rather dreamily. 'Sometimes, just walking down the street, I see a child and I think – that's my son, my daughter. My line, as it were. It gives me a greater sense of satisfaction than you can possibly imagine.'

The man was starting to get carried away, Jardine thought. It was time to get things back to a more businesslike level. 'A couple named Cathy and Martin Adams are having a baby by donor insemination. Are you the father of that child too?'

Millar looked a trifle evasive for a moment. 'I can't really remember. I never kept records, you see.'

Jackie Reid let out a short, bitter laugh. Her tone betrayed her complete and utter sense of disbelief. '*Your* children – *your* line – and you didn't keep any records?' she demanded aggressively. 'You don't expect us to believe that, do you, Dr Millar?'

The man looked a little sheepish at having been caught out. Somewhat reluctantly, he unlocked a drawer in his desk and drew out a small black notebook. He handed it across to Jardine. 'They're all in there – listed by age, rather than alphabetical order,' he admitted. 'Not all the addresses, of course. My children are rather widely scattered.'

Jardine flipped through the pages of the book, marvelling at the dozens of names without really reading them. He came, finally, to the most recent entries. One particular name almost leapt off the page at him. 'Oh my God,' Jardine muttered heavily, in a slow, ponderous tone, his face paling with shock.

'What is it, Mike?' Jackie asked, with sudden concern. She moved across the room towards him.

Looking stunned and miserable, Jardine handed her the notebook without a word. Jackie took it, running her eyes down the open page and finally finding the entry which had elicited his depressive reaction. Finally, Jackie understood, and shared it.

For dated three months previously, and written in a clear, bold hand, was the name Xavier Livingstone.

Chapter Twelve

McVitie's office was serving as a temporary conference room. Taggart, Jardine, Jackie Reid and two uniformed constables were seated around McVitie's desk, which had been cleared of all extraneous paperwork for an emergency discussion of the Millar case. McVitie himself looked harassed to the point of persecution. 'I thought we'd all better be prepared for the next twenty-four hours,' McVitie told them all. 'You don't really need me to tell you that all hell is going to break loose when the press and the public get hold of this. This station is going to be the centre of a national, if not an international, scandal.'

'I suppose there's no chance of keeping it from the media, sir,' Jardine enquired hopefully. McVitie shot him a scornful glare by way of an answer.

'So what's the official view?' Taggart wanted to know.

McVitie shook his head. 'God only knows, Jim. I've been on to the Procurator Fiscal's office and they haven't even got a clue what to charge him with at this stage.'

'Well, if they haven't, I sure don't,' Taggart grumbled.

'What about fraud, sir,' Jackie Reid suggested helpfully. 'False representation?'

McVitie shrugged. 'There's just never been a crime remotely like this in this country, to the best of my knowledge. In fact, no one seems quite sure if it's technically a crime at all.'

'Actually, it's worse, sir,' Jardine said. 'I've been on to the British Medical Association and they say that a donor should not be used for more than a handful of sperm donations. Otherwise there could be too many offspring with the same father in the community. They might, unknowingly, grow up and marry each other – with the danger of congenital defects in any children they might have.'

'Plus, of course, all regular donors have to be very carefully screened,' Jackie added. 'I think we can take it as a fairly safe assumption that Dr Millar didn't bother to screen himself.'

'Closer to home, does this case have any bearing whatsoever on Joan Mathieson's murder?' McVitie wanted to know. He stared directly at Taggart.

'It's difficult to draw any direct connection,' Taggart admitted. 'But the Adams are on that list, and I don't think we can afford to just ignore it.'

McVitie's office door suddenly burst open. Rob Gibson stormed in without knocking, his face black with anger. Ignoring Superintendent McVitie and Taggart, he faced Jardine squarely. 'Is it true, the rumour which is flying about in the outer office?' he demanded.

Taggart could have been furious at the rude intrusion, but he couldn't find it in himself to censure the young man. Instead, he just muttered softly: 'Stay out of it right now, Rob.'

But Gibson was past the point of appeasement. His voice rose to an angry shout. 'Dammit, I demand to know,' he thundered. 'I have a right to know who the father of my baby is.' He looked round the group of awkward, embarrassed faces. 'It's him, isn't it? It's that bastard Millar.'

Their silence gave him all the answer he needed. Gibson pivoted on the balls of his feet and stormed out of the office again, slamming the door behind him.

Taggart let out a long, low whistle of exhaled breath, glancing at McVitie. 'And that's just the reaction of a fairly level-headed, trained young officer,' he muttered heavily. 'I think you hit the nail on the head when you said all hell was going to break loose, sir.'

Perhaps predictably, Martin Adams' reaction was even more extreme. With insufficient evidence to charge him, Taggart had had no choice but to release him pending further enquiries. Jardine and Jackie Reid had escorted him home so that they could break the news to him and his wife together.

'I'll kill the bastard!' Adams raged, his face twisted with fury.

'You're in enough trouble already, Martin,' Jackie reminded him, pointedly, as Cathy clutched at his arm, trying to calm him down.

'Does it really matter?' she asked, trying to accept the news as philosophically as possible.

Martin stared at her blankly, still choked up with anger. 'What the hell do you mean, Cathy? Does it matter?'

'Nothing has really changed,' Cathy pointed out. 'Instead of the donor being anonymous, we know who the father is now. I still carried him, he's still going to be our baby.'

The suggestion seemed to enrage Adams even more. 'But he's not, is he?' he demanded aggressively. 'He's not going to be *our* baby. He's going to be yours . . . and *his*. Just think what your bloody mother would have made of that.'

Cathy's face fell as though she had been physically slapped. 'Don't talk about her like that,' she sobbed.

Jardine was feeling increasingly embarrassed, being in the middle of a domestic row. 'Look, you could always consider taking professional counselling,' he suggested, trying to defuse the situation.

It didn't work. Adams turned on him angrily. 'Professional counselling?' he demanded bitterly. 'We *had* professional counselling, dammit. From the man who did this. Now why the hell don't you just get out and leave us alone?'

There really wasn't an answer to that, Jardine realised. It was time to beat a hasty tactical retreat, he decided. A last word of warning seemed in order, however. 'Look, just don't do anything stupid,' he told Adams. He turned towards Jackie, flashing discreet signals that it was time to back off.

He was silent until they were safely outside the house. 'Well, I'm glad that little job is over,' he muttered thankfully, as they walked down the drive towards the car. 'I hate these messy domestic affairs.'

Jackie nodded thoughtfully, a slightly rueful smile on her lips. 'Perhaps we ought to count ourselves lucky,' she pointed out. 'Poor old Taggart has got to break the news to Peter Livingstone.'

That particularly unpleasant task was nearer than Jackie Reid realised. At that very moment, a stressed and weary Taggart had just walked in his own front door to discover Jean cradling the sleeping Xavier in her arms. Peter and Marta Livingstone were seated by the fireplace, drinking cups of tea.

Jean Taggart placed a finger to her lips, warning him to keep quiet. She smiled up at him. 'Isn't this nice?' she whispered. 'Peter and Marta popped in to pay us a visit.'

Taken by surprise, Taggart found it impossible to keep a look of dismay from showing on his face. Livingstone could not help but notice, immediately misinterpreting it. He pushed himself to his feet, hastily making excuses. 'Actually, we really have to get going now,' he muttered awkwardly. 'We have to get home to put Xavier to bed.'

It was Taggart's turn to feel awkward, realising that Livingstone had jumped to the wrong conclusion. He tried to force a smile, but it just wouldn't come. Instead, he could only regard Livingstone gravely. 'No, please, Peter – don't go yet,' he urged. He turned to his wife. 'Look, Jean – why don't you take Marta out to the kitchen and fix us all some supper? I'd like to talk to Peter alone for a few minutes.'

Jean flashed him a questioning look, but chose not to argue. She knew her husband well enough to recognise that certain look on his face. Whatever was on his mind was important, and he would no doubt explain further in his own good time. She held up the sleeping baby as Marta rose to take him. The two women left the room.

Livingstone stared closely at Taggart's strained face. 'You look as though you've had a rough day,' he observed.

Taggart let out a sigh. 'It's not over yet,' he muttered heavily. He crossed to the drinks cabinet, pausing to look back at Livingstone. 'Can Marta drive, by the way?'

Livingstone nodded. 'Yes – why?' he asked, sounding slightly puzzled.

'Because I think you're going to need a very stiff drink,' Taggart told him. He poured out two extremely large measures of whisky and carried them across to the fireplace.

'What's this in aid of, Jim?' Livingstone asked, accepting his drink.

Taggart's face reflected his embarrassment, and the delicacy of the situation. He eyed Livingstone awkwardly. 'Look, Peter – I always used to be like a father figure to you,' he started, uncertainly.

Livingstone laughed, cutting him short. 'Jim, you might have been a lot of things to me, but a father figure was never one of them,' he said, with more than a trace of humour in his tone.

Taggart took a healthy slug of whisky from his glass. He tried again. 'Hell, Peter – this is very difficult for me, I want you to understand that,' he muttered.

The smile faded from Livingstone's face as he realised how serious Taggart really was. 'Come on, Jim – out with it,' he urged.

'There's something I have to tell you,' Taggart went

on. 'Something which, as a friend, I feel you deserve to know before you see it splashed all over the papers tomorrow morning.'

'Papers?' Livingstone echoed blankly.

Taggart took a breath. 'The Millar Fertility Clinic,' he blurted out. 'I believe you and Marta went to it.'

A look of shock crossed Livingstone's face, shortly followed by anger. 'How the hell do you know that?' he demanded.

Taggart shrugged. 'That's not important. The point is – '

Livingstone cut the explanation short. 'No, the point is that I asked you and Jean to be the godparents of my child, not for you to go probing into my private life,' he said angrily.

Taggart let the man's rage wash over him. He waited until Livingstone had lapsed into a sullen silence before going on. 'Please, Peter – let me explain,' he pleaded. 'I know that Xavier was conceived by donor insemination, but there's something you don't know.'

'You bastard,' Livingstone hissed at him. He slammed his drink down on the mantelpiece. Reaching down to the chair for his coat, he snatched it up angrily. 'Just forget you ever saw me again, Jim. And make my apologies to Jean. We're leaving.' He began to stride towards the door.

'Dr Millar is the father of your child,' Taggart called after him.

Livingstone stopped in his tracks. He turned, slowly, staring at Taggart in total shock. 'What?'

Taggart's shoulders slumped, now that it was out in the open. 'Dr Millar fathered Xavier,' he repeated, softly. 'Along with Rob Gibson's baby and about sixty other youngsters in the Glasgow area.' He shrugged his shoulders helplessly. 'I just thought you ought to know, that's all.'

Taggart walked over to the fireplace and picked up Livingstone's glass, holding it out to him again. 'Here, finish your drink. There's more in the bottle.'

Chapter Thirteen

As fully expected, the Millar case was front-page news in most of the national newspapers the next morning. Headlines ranged from the fairly restrained 'SEX CLINIC SCANDAL' in one of the more conservative dailies, to 'SCOTLAND'S SUPER-STUD' in one of the more lurid tabloids.

By 8.30 a.m., an angry mob of parents – mostly fathers – had started to gather outside the Millar Fertility Clinic, baying for blood. By nine, shouted insults and threats had turned to more open violence, with bricks being hurled through windows and at least one concerted attempt to smash the front door down. Five police cars and sixteen uniformed officers were hastily despatched to the scene, finally restoring some sort of order shortly before midday.

The gentlemen of the press, meanwhile, being more experienced in such matters, had largely ignored the clinic, going straight to the heart of the matter at the Millars' private residence. There was a mob of at least thirty reporters and photographers besieging the house as Jardine and Jackie Reid arrived shortly before one in the afternoon. Trying to ignore the barrage of flashguns and shouted questions, they battled their way through the crowd to the front door. It was opened, extremely cautiously, by Ruth Millar, who had been peering anxiously through the downstairs curtains every few minutes since they had first been woken in the early hours of the morning.

Jardine and Jackie edged their way quickly inside the house, helping Ruth Millar to close the door again against the surging crowd of pressmen. She led them through to the lounge, where Dr Millar sat in a high-backed chair, turned away from the curtained windows. Ruth motioned for Jardine and Jackie to sit themselves down, then took up a position near her husband. Outwardly, at least, she gave the appearance of supporting him, Jardine thought, reflecting as men frequently do what strangely unpredictable creatures women could be.

There was no point in beating about the bush. Jardine came straight to the point. 'While the PF decides what charges to bring against you, Dr Millar, I suggest that you and your wife get as far away from Glasgow as you can. For your own safety.'

'Can't the police give us protection?' Ruth Millar asked, looking worried.

Jackie raised one eyebrow. 'Against sixty furious husbands who would like to lynch your husband? We'd need a SWAT team.' She turned to Millar. 'Now, do you have somewhere you could go, somewhere to lay low for a few days?'

Millar thought for a while. 'Some friends of ours have a holiday cottage near Loch Ness,' he murmured. 'Would that be far enough away, do you think?'

Millar himself seemed to be quite happy about the idea, but Ruth was still indignant. 'It's not right that we should be forced to live like fugitives,' she protested.

Millar reached out to pat her hand, quelling her objections. 'Look, it'll just be for a short while – until my trial comes up,' he assured her. He glanced up at Jardine. 'There *will* be a trial, I take it?'

Jardine nodded. 'Almost certainly.'

Millar considered things for a while. 'We'll make arrangements and leave tonight,' he said finally, as casually as if he was planning a weekend leisure trip. 'In the meantime, is there any chance of the police clearing away all those photographers that seem to be camped outside? I really don't want my picture splashed all over the papers.'

'We'll do what we can,' Jardine said, purposely non-committal. It was not something he would care to promise. He turned to leave, suddenly remembering the other reason for their visit. 'By the way, Dr Millar – you were at the church the other day when Joan Mathieson was taken ill, weren't you?'

Millar nodded. 'That's right. She was Cathy Adams' mother, I believe.'

'You never met her?' Jardine asked.

'No.' Millar was quite adamant. 'But I believe my wife spoke to her.'

'Only briefly,' Ruth put in quickly. 'Outside the church, just before we all went in for the service. Cathy seemed very anxious to introduce her mother to everybody.'

Jackie Reid had a question of her own. She addressed it to Millar. 'Being a doctor, did it not occur to you to go to her aid when she was taken ill?'

Millar looked at her in surprise. 'I was at the christening of one of my children,' he said, almost indignantly. 'It was a very special moment for me.'

Ruth Millar noticed the look of contempt which came over Jackie's face. She rose to her feet, shielding her husband protectively. 'Now please – if there are no more questions, would you mind leaving us alone?' she asked. Without waiting for an answer, she led the way to the front door. As she opened it, the mob of pressmen surged forward again.

Jardine jumped out on to the front step, brandishing his warrant card like a magic talisman. 'Back,' he shouted, authoritatively. Surprisingly, it worked – just long enough for he and Jackie to get out of the house and Ruth to shut and bolt the door again. He grinned as the media people recovered themselves and began to press forward again. 'Why not give them a break, fellers?' he suggested. 'Did none of you ever want to be a father?'

Two hours had passed since Jardine and Jackie Reid had left. Ruth Millar walked over to the window again, parting the curtains cautiously and peeping out momentarily.

'Are they still there?' Millar asked.

Ruth closed the curtains again, stepping back from the window. 'Like vultures,' she confirmed with a nod.

There was a long and heavy silence in the room. Finally Millar looked up at his wife, a look of contrition on his face. 'Ruth – I'm sorry,' he said lamely.

Ruth stared at him for several moments. 'That's it, is it?' she wanted to know. 'You destroy our careers, cause untold misery, and you say sorry.'

Millar hung his head abjectly. 'I just couldn't help myself,' he muttered. 'It was all so easy to start with. A dozen children – who would ever have known?'

Ruth laughed bitterly. 'So why didn't you stop?' She paused, reflectively. 'I suppose there was always a question at the back of my mind, perhaps even a suspicion. I always wondered why you had to be at every christening.' She turned away, almost embarrassed to face him. 'Would it have made any difference if I'd been able to have children?' she went on, in a sad little voice.

'Possibly,' Millar told her after a while.

Ruth sighed. 'So it's my fault?'

'I didn't say that,' her husband muttered miserably. His face brightened suddenly, showing the ghost of a smile as he looked up at her again. 'Look, Ruth – our marriage has been wonderful, I mean that. We never needed children, ever. The clinic seemed to make up for it.'

Ruth seemed to grasp the full irony of the situation for the first time. 'Oh yes – you made sure of that, didn't you?' she observed, cynically. She broke off, shaking her head in sheer disbelief. 'My God, Colin – when I think of the marriages you must have ruined. The couples out there who are probably tearing themselves apart right now because of your selfishness. The children who are going to grow up despised and hated because of what you are. Did you ever for one minute stop to think about *that*?'

Millar began to sob, tears running down his cheeks.

Ruth looked at him, torn with the mixed emotions of pity, affection and bitterness which churned inside her. Colin was so much a child himself, in many ways. Finally, bitterness won the day. 'Don't cry for us, Colin,' Ruth told him coldly. 'Cry for them.'

Chapter Fourteen

The mood in the pub, which had started by being merely heated, was now turning distinctly ugly, as the men's anger was fuelled by the increasing doses of Dutch courage they had consumed throughout the evening. There were over twenty fathers present, including Peter Livingstone, Rob Gibson and Martin Adams. The assembly, which had ostensibly started out as a show of solidarity along the lines of a victim support group, was rapidly turning into a mob. Thoughts of mere protest were already long-forgotten and swamped under increasing calls for more direct and violent action. Individuals no longer called for justice, they demanded revenge. And individuality itself was rapidly being sucked in to the hungry maw of mob rule.

Peter Livingstone seemed to have appointed himself

some sort of a spokesman for the group. He was more than a little drunk, his face flushed and excited. 'I'm telling you, tonight will be our last chance,' he shouted above the general roar of conversation. 'I know the way the police mind works, and right now they'll be planning to move Millar out to a safe house under cover of darkness.' He turned towards Rob Gibson for confirmation. 'Isn't that right, Rob?'

Gibson was in a more rational frame of mind, having drunk a lot less than the others. He was also acutely aware of his own personal, and highly delicate, position. He regarded the sea of angry faces with growing concern before turning his attention to Livingstone. 'Look, I'm a serving police officer. I can't be a part of a bloody lynch mob.'

Livingstone gave him a scathing glance. 'It wouldn't have stopped me,' he boasted, the drink speaking for him.

Gibson eyed him questioningly. 'Wouldn't it?' he muttered, doubtfully. He turned his attention to the mob at large, appealing to them. 'Listen, all of you – just think on it for a moment. Just think of what it is you're all talking about here.'

He was greeted with a chorus of jeers. From a nearby table, a large, burly ex-docker called Sam Jackson rose to his feet, swaying noticeably. 'Bloody Millar didn't stop to think what he was doing,' he muttered thickly. He looked round at his colleagues. 'Isn't that right, lads?'

The mob spoke, with its single voice. 'Aye!' Everyone looked towards Livingstone again, waiting for a lead. He supplied it, fired up on his own sense of outrage and the backing of his private army. 'We spent a fortune on fertility treatment – all of us,' he told them. 'For some of you it probably represented your life savings. We were hoping to buy hopes, dreams, but we were cheated. How many of us can honestly say that our marriages are going to survive this thing?'

The crowd erupted into a fresh roar of approval. Jackson climbed up onto a chair, waving his pint in the air in a rallying gesture. 'He's right, lads – so what are we bloody waiting for?' he shouted at the top of his voice. Throwing the last of his beer down his throat, Jackson jumped to the floor. It was the signal for everyone to hastily finish their drinks and lurch to their feet.

Only Rob Gibson remained seated. He reached up, clutching at Livingstone's sleeve. 'For God's sake, think of the consequences,' he pleaded.

Livingstone sneered at him. '*You* sit here and think of the consequences,' he said bitterly. 'We already have.'

There was a clatter of beer glasses being slammed down on tables as the angry crowd surged towards the door. Rob Gibson remained seated, gazing moodily down at his own unfinished beer and fighting to come to terms with the inner conflict which tore at his mind and body. There was an almost physical itch in his legs which made him want to jump to his feet and go with the mob, but it was counterbalanced by a feeling of leadenness in his shoulders. Part of his mind screamed out for revenge, the exultant thrill of retribution, but this in turn was held in check by something which Gibson was unable, or unwilling, to identify as caution or cowardice.

He listened to the sound of people piling into cars outside the pub, of doors being slammed, engines started up and revved menacingly. Then, finally, the burden of choice was removed from him as the cars began to move away, the sound of their engines and blaring horns fading away into the distance.

Ruth Millar looked up from packing the last suitcase in alarm as the noise of the approaching convoy came to her ears. She crossed to the window, staring out over the heads of the waiting press photographers as the first car drew up outside the house.

There was a sudden flurry of excitement and activity as the journalists, bored and frustrated with their long and totally unproductive wait, reacted to this promising new development. In a feverish mass, they surged towards the gates as the rest of the cars pulled up and disgorged their shouting, jeering occupants in front of the Millar residence.

'What is it? What's going on?' Millar asked his wife nervously. He was already dressed to leave, wearing a heavy black scarf around his neck ready to throw over his head as a protection against prying cameras.

Ruth turned towards her husband, the beginnings of fear showing on her face. She was in little doubt as to the intentions of the mob, and the single policeman who had been placed on duty outside the house offered scant protection. As if to confirm her fears, a brick came crashing through the window behind her, showering her hair with splintered glass. 'My God – they're attacking us,' she sobbed in terror. She rushed across the room to the sofa, throwing her weight against it. She looked across at Millar with desperation in her eyes. 'Come on, give me a hand. We have to barricade the door.'

Outside, pandemonium reigned as the mob of enraged husbands swept up against the crowd of delighted press photographers. Hardly able to believe their luck that such a juicy story had just dropped into their laps, they surged forwards, flashbulbs and light guns popping off like a small-scale firework display. The mob, fronted by Livingstone, Adams and Jackson, swept them aside roughly. At least half a dozen fist fights broke out spontaneously, with snatched cameras hastily converted into highly expensive missiles to be hurled at the windows of the Millar house.

In the thick of the mêlée, the uniformed constable struggled to keep himself from being swamped, let alone restore order. Identifying Livingstone as the leader, he forced his way in front of him, making a vain appeal for common sense. 'Come on, lads, you'll achieve nothing this way,' he shouted impotently. 'Just turn around and go home, like sensible adults.'

His appeal went unheeded. Livingstone merely stepped around him as Martin Adams shoulder-charged the young constable out of the way. He unhooked his police radio from his uniform, preparing to put in an emergency appeal for reinforcements. Jackson snatched the radio from his hands, hurling it against the wall of the house. 'Do yourself a favour, son,' he snarled. 'Just get out of the way and don't try to stop us. It's Millar we want.'

Still led by Livingstone, the mob swarmed up the drive towards the front of the house as the press photographers fell back to a more safe and convenient vantage-point. They continued taking photographs as a group of six husbands began to kick the front door in, and several others began to ransack the garden for stones and other suitable implements of destruction. Nobody paid the slightest attention to the totally impotent constable who ran wildly amongst them, shouting out desperately for someone with a mobile phone.

Ruth Millar screamed as the sound of ripping and splintering wood echoed up the corridor from the front entrance. Seconds later, burly shoulders were thumping against the inner door of the lounge. The sofa began to slide back across the carpeted floor as sheer weight of numbers forced the door open.

Then the mob was in the room at last. The men froze, temporarily, identifying their prey, who cowered against the far wall, regarding them with the frightened gaze of a trapped animal.

Bravely, Ruth Millar stood her ground, facing them defiantly. 'Get out of here – all of you,' she shouted, in a surprisingly strong voice.

Livingstone stepped forward, taking her by the shoulders and pinning her arms to her sides in a firm but gentle grip. 'Please don't get in our way, Mrs Millar,' he said, almost apologetically. 'We don't mean you any harm, believe me. It's just your husband we want.' He pulled her gently aside, clearing the way for his followers to advance on the terrified figure of Colin Millar. The man threw his arms up around his face in a useless attempt at self-protection, trying to bury his body in the wall.

Livingstone continued to hold Ruth Millar as each man in turn stepped forward to deliver his own personal retribution. Martin Adams got to him first, slamming his knee into Millar's groin, causing the man to double up with a shriek of agony. Adams reached down to haul him up again, pinning him against the wall. 'Maybe you won't be so bloody fertile after we've finished with you,' he threatened. He held the sagging man upright as Jackson moved into position, swinging a curving right hook to the side of the man's head. 'That's for one,' he grunted, then pulled back his arm for another punch. 'And that's for twins,' he spat out, slamming his fist low into Millar's solar plexus.

The first two blows set the pattern for an almost ritual attack, in which each man took his shot and then held the victim in place for further punishment. Millar's face was covered in blood now, both eyes half-closed with puffy swellings. He seemed barely conscious, and probably unable to stand on his own feet, yet time and time again someone else hauled him upright and the beatings continued, each one accompanied by a roar of encouragement from the mob.

Above the din, the wail of police sirens could suddenly be heard from outside the house. Moments later, there was the sound of screeching tyres, opening and closing car doors and the sound of heavy footsteps pounding up the driveway.

Livingstone whirled towards the door as the first of a dozen uniformed officers swarmed into the room. He was one of the first to be grabbed, and accepted his capture calmly and without struggling. His single regret at that moment was that he hadn't got round to taking his punch. He allowed himself to be dragged bodily out of the house, his arms firmly pinioned behind his back. As he reached the gate, another police car was just drawing to a halt. Jardine and Jackie Reid climbed out, looking round at the scene in total dismay.

Jardine's eyes fell on Livingstone. His angry glare was returned by a triumphant, drunken smirk.

Jardine stepped forward, jabbing his forefinger right under Livingstone's nose. 'You're nicked,' he hissed in Livingstone's face.

Taggart strode through the prisoner-holding area, reviewing the previous night's catch. Passing three of the cells, each containing a half-dozen errant husbands, he eventually came upon Livingstone, who had been locked up on his own. Taggart beckoned to the custody sergeant, who unlocked the cell to let him in.

Livingstone sat on the edge of one of the lower bunks, cradling his head in his hands and looking thoroughly dejected. Taggart wondered briefly whether it was remorse or simply the effects of a raging hangover. He looked up at Taggart sullenly, waiting to see what the man's reaction would be. Taggart's anger was tempered with a certain amount of compassion. '*You* should have know better,' he said simply.

Livingstone glowered at him. 'You had no right to keep me in here,' he complained.

Taggart grunted. 'I had every right,' he pointed out. 'Conspiracy, assault, obstructing a police officer in the course of his duty, forcible entry, malicious damage . . .' He paused for a moment. 'Did I miss anything out, Peter?'

'I never even got to touch him,' Livingstone protested, seizing on the single defence he had.

Taggart sighed heavily. 'I should throw the book at you,' he muttered.

Livingstone shrugged. 'So go ahead. A fine present to give your godson.'

Taggart sank down on the bed opposite, with another deep sigh. 'For God's sake – what got *into* you?' he demanded.

The look of sullen defiance faded from Livingstone's face, leaving him looking merely wretched. 'Have you got any idea how it feels not being able to give your wife the child she wants so much?' he asked. 'And then to be betrayed by the very doctor you trusted?'

Taggart nodded his head slowly, sympathising with the man's problem but not quite able to accept his solution. 'It was still no reason to take the law into your own hands,' he pointed out.

Livingstone was defiant again. 'I'd do it again, given half the chance,' he muttered.

Taggart glared at him, his anger rising. 'You do and I'll have you hanged, drawn and quartered,' he threatened.

A faint, rueful smile crossed Livingstone's face. 'You always were a bully, Jim,' he said quietly. He paused momentarily. 'Do you know – I always wanted to say that to you when I was still in the force.'

Taggart eyed him philosophically. 'Maybe you should have done,' he observed. 'You might regret saying it now.' He rose from the bed and crossed to the door, nodding over to the custody sergeant to let him out of the cell. He returned upstairs, popping his head round the door of Jardine's office just in time to catch him hauling Rob Gibson over the coals. 'What's the problem?' Taggart asked.

Jardine's face was grave as he nodded at Gibson. 'He knew what they were planning, sir – and he did nothing.'

Gibson looked up, appealing directly to Taggart. 'They tried to involve me, sir.'

Jardine whirled on the young DC, his voice rising to a shout. 'You *were* involved, dammit.' He repeated his earlier accusation. 'You knew what they were planning to do, yet you did nothing.'

Gibson faced Jardine directly. 'Yes, I did *nothing*,' he said, with heavy emphasis. 'At least I can tell that to my kid in twenty years' time when he's old enough to understand. I did nothing – and I'm proud of it.'

Taggart shook his head, with an expression of total exasperation on his face. 'This place is turning into a madhouse,' he muttered. He jabbed his finger in Gibson's direction. 'And you are looking at suspension,' he growled, before ducking out of the door and stamping off to his own private office.

Chapter Fifteen

The lochside cottage was a haven of rural peace as Colin and Ruth Millar drove up in their respective cars. Ruth jumped out, opening the boot of her car and starting to haul out the heavy suitcases. She looked over towards her husband, who remained in his vehicle with the side window half open.

'Well – are you going to get out and give me a hand?' Ruth demanded.

Millar looked furtively out through the window. 'Can you just make sure there aren't any press people around?' he asked, nervously.

Ruth shot him a scornful glance, then dragged the two suitcases out of the boot and began to carry them towards the cottage. 'They're probably all lurking behind the trees,' she called over her shoulder, sarcastically.

Warily, Millar climbed out, retrieving his own bags from the back seat. Still casting anxious glances from side to side, he made his way up to the cottage door as his wife opened it, ducking over the portal like a rabbit seeking the sanctuary of its burrow.

It was more of a cabin than a cottage, consisting merely of a single bedroom, an open living area and a kitchenette. Ruth Millar dropped her cases in the middle of the floor and stood up straight, sweeping her hands around the place in a grand gesture. 'Well, this is prison,' she announced, rather depressingly. 'You'd better start getting used to it.' She walked across to the single large window and drew the curtains, gazing out over the shimmering waters of the loch. 'Actually, as prisons go, it's got a nice view,' she added as an after-thought.

'It may not come to that,' Millar muttered, although his tone did not carry much conviction.

Ruth turned away from the window to face him, a somewhat bitter smile on her face. 'Don't kid yourself, Colin. They'll find something to charge you with. You'll probably make legal history.'

Millar was silent for a while, considering this scenario. He stared at his wife through sad and soulful eyes, like a frightened little boy. 'Will you wait for me . . . if I do?' he asked uncertainly.

It was Ruth's turn to consider things. There was doubt in her eyes as she looked at him. 'I don't know,' she admitted honestly, at length. 'I'm not even sure how I feel about you at the moment, let alone what I will think in a few months' time.'

Millar looked as though he was going to start crying again. He shuffled awkwardly towards his wife, reaching out for her. Ruth turned her back on him abruptly, staring out of the window again. 'Don't touch me – please,' she called over her shoulder, in a firm, warning voice.

Millar stopped in his tracks, lowering his out-stretched arms to his sides. The fear of rejection showed on his face. 'But I need you more than ever now, Ruth,' he murmured, wretchedly. He moved up to stand beside her at the window, but keeping his distance. 'Look, we can make a fresh start, put all this behind us,' he suggested hopefully.

Ruth let out a little snort of derision. 'Doing what, exactly?' she asked scornfully. 'Running a little corner grocery shop in the Outer Hebrides? Face up to reality, Colin, for God's sake. Nobody will ever employ us again. Our careers are over. This thing will probably follow us around for the rest of our lives.'

Millar shrugged faintly, desperately seeking hope and clutching at straws. 'We could always change our names. It's easy enough to do.'

Ruth turned to face him directly, with a weary, resigned expression on her face. 'Listen, Colin – if you want to live in dreams and hopes, then go ahead. But just don't expect me to respond with boundless enthusiasm. Right now, I just need time to do a lot of thinking.' She paused briefly before delivering the punchline to this little speech. 'Which is why I'm not going to be here a lot of the time.'

It took a moment for this last piece of information to sink in. When it did, Millar looked devastated. 'Please, Ruth – you're not going to leave me here on my own?'

She regarded him coldly. 'Someone's got to look after the clinic, all the equipment – even though it is closed.' A slightly incredulous expression crossed her face. 'Surely you didn't imagine that I was just going to sit around here for weeks on end?'

From the look of shock on his face, it was obvious that he had. 'What am I going to do?' he asked eventually, in a weak little voice.

Ruth shrugged carelessly, unable to dredge up the faintest degree of compassion for the man. As she had already tried to explain, her true feelings were still unclear in her head, all jumbled up with a hotch-potch of mixed emotions and her personal sense of betrayal. Part of her wanted desperately to hurt him, as deeply as he had hurt her. 'Enjoy the peace and quiet,' she told him. 'Make the most of it. In a few months' time, when your face is all over the news and you're looking out at life from the wrong side of a prison cell, this might seem like paradise.'

She turned away from the window and started unpacking the suitcases, leaving Millar standing there stunned, shocked and confused. Was she deliberately being cruel, he wondered – or was she merely trying to prepare him for what might lie ahead? They were questions to which Millar did not have the answers, although there was one thing he did know. He had relied on Ruth's strength for so long, as a prop against his own, essential weakness, that he was not sure he could survive without her now.

Jackie Reid had completely cleared the main notice-board in the outer office, and was now busily redecorating it with pinned-up photographs of babies, toddlers and young children, watched by a fascinated Jardine.

Taggart emerged from his private office and

approached them. 'By the way, I want you both to lay off Martin Adams,' he muttered.

Jardine stared at him incredulously. It was not like Taggart to back away from a hunch. 'You mean you want to let him off the hook, sir?'

Taggart flashed him a slightly reproving glance. 'I didn't say that, Michael. I said just don't pressure him – for a while, at least. We need hard evidence against him, and that's the one thing we haven't got.'

'But you still think he's guilty, sir?' Jackie Reid asked.

Taggart was noncommittal. 'I still think this is a *family* murder,' he said firmly. It was an oddly qualified statement, Jackie thought.

Taggart turned his attention back to Jardine, handing him a sheet of paper. 'Now, Joan Mathieson had a brother and one son living locally, as well as two others who are overseas. I want you to contact them, talk to them, find out as much as you can.' He studied Jackie's photo display closely for the first time. 'What's all this? Running a bonny baby competition, are we?'

Jackie Reid smiled proudly, pleased that Taggart had seen fit to at least make passing reference to her handiwork, which had been entirely her own idea. 'They're all Millar's children, sir,' she explained. 'I got them from the parents. Even if they don't help us in any way, at least they brighten the place up.'

Taggart did not look too impressed. He fished a small bunch of keys out of his pocket and tossed them towards her. 'There's the keys to Joan Mathieson's cottage near Perth. You can brighten *me* up by going up there and turfing out any clues you can. Anything which will give us a better idea of her relationships with her children. Letters, personal papers, perhaps even a will if we're lucky.'

Jackie nodded, getting the general idea. 'I'll do it right away, sir,' she promised.

'Good.' Taggart took one last glance at the photo display before leaving to go back to his office. 'Ugly-looking lot, aren't they?' he observed cynically.

Chapter Sixteen

Jardine found Tom Fleming up at the back of the old cemetery, busily hacking back overgrown hedgerows with a power saw as his nephew, Ian, gathered up the fallen branches and scrub and fed them into the gaping funnel of a huge, trailer-mounted shredder. The noise was deafening, although neither man wore protective ear-muffs, Jardine noticed.

Fleming switched off the power saw as Jardine approached and flashed his ID card.

'Tom Fleming?' Jardine yelled at the top of his voice, above the continuing din of the shredder.

Fleming nodded, touching Jardine lightly on the shoulder and moving away towards a quieter part of the cemetery. Jardine followed him, waiting until they had reached a spot where normal conversation might just be possible.

'Aren't you afraid of waking the dead?' he asked eventually, jerking his head towards the rows of old and unkempt gravestones.

The facetious question raised a faint smile on Fleming's face. 'Och, they'll bide a while.' He looked at Jardine questioningly. 'What can I do for you, Inspector?'

'You're Joan Fleming's brother, is that right?' Jardine asked, pausing until a brief nod from Fleming confirmed this fact. 'I'm sorry about your sister,' he added, with a suitably apologetic expression.

Fleming merely shrugged. 'There's many who wouldn't be,' he muttered philosophically. 'She could be a poisonous woman, could Joan. Difficult to get on with, and more difficult to like. Still, all that said, I suppose she didn't deserve what happened to her.'

It was obvious that there had been little love lost between them, Jardine realised. 'Are you her only brother, Mr Fleming?' he asked.

'Aye, there was just the two of us,' Fleming confirmed. 'We were never really close, except when we were kids.'

'And her children?' Jardine asked. 'How did you get on with them?'

Fleming shrugged again. 'Well enough, I suppose. But they're all gone now, except for Cathy of course, and Ian over there.' He nodded over to the young man operating the shredder. 'He was the last one to leave home, after the others moved away. When he just couldn't abide living with her any longer, he came down here to work for me.' He broke off to pull a tobacco tin and packet of papers from his jacket pocket. Hand-rolling a cigarette, he glanced up at Jardine with a somewhat guilty, apologetic smile on his face. 'I suppose it's not very nice to speak ill of the dead, is it?'

It was not a question Jardine could answer for him, and he didn't try. 'I believe you were at the birthday party, when your sister made remarks about the baby not being Martin's?'

Fleming's expression hardened again. 'Aye, that was a cruel thing she did. She knew it was cruel, of course – but then she was never one to miss a stab in the back, for any of us.'

'Why?' Jardine asked bluntly. 'Do you know why your sister acted the way she did?'

Fleming finished rolling his cigarette, slipped it between his lips and lit it. He took a couple of slow, thoughtful draws. 'She was a very bitter woman, but then I suppose she had some cause to be,' he said. 'Her husband left her when she was twenty-eight, with four young children to bring up on her own.'

Jardine didn't understand. 'But surely that would have brought her closer to her children?' he pointed out.

Fleming smiled ruefully. 'Aye,' he agreed. 'That was the trouble. Joan's kids were everything to her – they were all she had. But one by one they grew up, developed lives of their own, met people and fell in love. She tried to cling on to them, of course – but they all left her in the end. She could never forgive them for that, you see.'

Jardine nodded understandingly as the picture started to make sense – or at least a slightly twisted sort of logic. 'But then why did Cathy invite her down to stay?' he asked Fleming.

The man grunted. 'That's a good question.'

'Do you have an answer?' Jardine prompted.

Fleming sucked on his thin cigarette again, thoughtfully. 'I suppose Cathy was always the closest to Joan, being the only daughter. And she was always big-hearted, was Cathy. I think that in the back of her mind, she honestly thought it would make Joan happy to see her grandchild born. She's never seen the others, of course – only photographs.' Fleming finished his cigarette and crushed it out between his finger and thumb, returning the extinguished stub to his tobacco tin. He smiled at Jardine apologetically. 'Will that be all, do you think? This is a new contract, and I've got a deadline to meet.'

Jardine nodded sympathetically. 'Of course. I just need to have a quick word with your nephew.' He turned and walked away towards the shredding machine, which was making more din than ever, with distinctly suspect mechanical noises adding to the grinding and crunching sounds of the whirling blades chewing up wood. Jardine was no mechanic, but he suspected the machine was on its last legs, or at least in urgent need of a good service. However, it still appeared to be doing its job quite efficiently, he thought as he approached the thundering machine. He was quite surprised at the size and thickness of the material it could apparently cope with. The ravenous monster quite happily gulped down branches up to three inches thick, spraying them out as a coarsely-textured pulp from the funnel on the far side of the machine.

Ian Mathieson continued heaping waste into the feeder as Jardine approached. He seemed quite unaffected by the noise, which was causing Jardine's eardrums actual physical pain. Clapping his hands over his ears, Jardine screamed out at the top of his voice: 'Do you mind turning that thing off for a moment?'

Ian looked at him in some surprise, but complied. He stopped topping up the feeder, allowed the shredder to munch through its current load and finally shut it down. It took Jardine's ears several seconds to adjust to the thundering sounds of silence.

Jardine introduced himself. 'I've just been talking to your uncle,' he explained finally. 'Now I just need to ask you a few questions about your mother, and her relationships with the family.'

Ian's expression was openly cynical. 'If you've talked to Uncle Tom, then there's probably not much I can tell you,' he muttered.

'I'll be the judge of that,' Jardine told him. 'Now, you stayed with her the longest, you must understand the way she was more than anyone.'

Ian nodded. 'Oh, I understood her all right,' he said bitterly. 'Basically, she just couldn't cope with the idea of any of us becoming independent.' He paused, looking at Jardine questioningly. 'Do you know, she missed my brother Angus's wedding completely – can you believe that?'

Jardine shrugged. 'Did she have a reason?'

Ian laughed. 'Oh, she said afterwards that she couldn't find the church – but we all knew she'd done it deliberately, just to make her point.'

Jardine consulted the brief notes Taggart had given him. 'Angus – that's the one in Australia, right?'

Ian nodded again. 'And Gavin, that's the one who went to Canada, she went to his wedding but ignored his wife all the way through it.'

'What about Cathy's wedding?' Jardine asked.

Ian shrugged. 'Cathy's different. Mum kept in with her, despite making it obvious that she hated Martin.'

'Do you know why she was particularly antagonistic towards Martin?' Jardine wanted to know.

Ian looked at him in surprise. 'Isn't it obvious? She resented Martin because he was successful and well-off. It was a sort of jealousy, I suppose.' He was silent for a while, a wistful look on his face as he thought back. 'You have to remember that we all had to struggle after our father ran out on us. I grew up wearing my brothers' cast-off clothes and shoes.' Ian returned to the present, eyeing Jardine almost defiantly. 'But she was our Mum, whatever else she was. No one in our family killed her, if that's what you think.'

'She wasn't Martin's mum,' Jardine pointed out, studying the young man's face carefully for a reaction.

Ian didn't even think about it. He shook his head vehemently. 'Martin wouldn't have done it. He loves Cathy too much.'

Jardine was thoughtful for a while. It was obvious that he was not going to get any evidence against Martin Adams from this source, he realised. Ian was firmly in defence of the man – possibly out of a sense of loyalty to his sister, Jardine thought. 'And what about your two brothers – are they going to come over for the funeral?' he asked, looking for new avenues of exploration.

Ian treated Jardine to one of his cynical, questioning smiles. 'Would you travel halfway round the world for one?' he asked.

'If it was my mother, then yes,' Jardine answered honestly. 'Besides, I saw some of the birthday greetings video your brother Angus sent over. He seemed quite fond of your mother.'

Ian laughed openly. 'Yes, it was quite convincing, wasn't it? But you obviously missed the point of that entire little charade.'

'Charade?' Jardine queried, puzzled again.

'The birthday party, the family get-together – all that happy families video stuff with the kids being forced to sing Happy Birthday Grandma. Did you think that was all for Mum's benefit?' Ian asked him.

Jardine shrugged. 'Who else?'

Ian gave him a secretive, confiding grin. 'It wasn't for Mum. It was for Cathy,' he told Jardine.

Chapter Seventeen

Jackie Reid pulled up outside Joan Mathieson's Perthshire cottage and climbed out of the car, looking up and down the deserted country road and marvelling at the isolation of the place. Apart from one small bungalow a couple of hundred yards away, there were no other signs of habitation besides a few cows grazing in a nearby field.

Jackie closed the car door and pushed open the small wooden gate, taking the keys Taggart had given her out of her pocket. She approached the front door of the cottage, opened it and let herself in.

She was immediately impressed with the neatness of the place as she wandered down the short hallway, peering briefly into the two rooms which made up the downstairs floor. Everything looked not only spotlessly clean, but also almost clinically tidy. There was not a single piece of furniture which did not appear to be precisely in the place it ought to be, no clutter of any kind, nothing left lying around. It was all almost too perfect Jackie thought.

There was something else, something odd about the general decor, Jackie sensed as she walked into the living-room for a more detailed look round. It was a niggling little detail which made the room seem strange. It took her several moments to identify what it was, but when things finally clicked, Jackie was intrigued. For the sense of oddness was conveyed not by the presence of anything in the room but by its absence. There was something missing from the scene – something which any normal person would have expected to find in the home of an elderly woman who had borne four children.

There were no photographs! No framed snapshots of children or grandchildren adorning the walls or mantelpiece. Nothing, in fact, to suggest that the cottage had ever been a family home.

Still pondering on this anomaly, Jackie crossed the room to an old-fashioned bureau-cum-writing desk in the corner by the fireplace and pulled the flap open. There were a couple of pens, a few sheets of writing paper and a small bundle of letters, held together with a rubber band. Jackie pushed them to one side for the moment, opening one of the bureau drawers in search of more official papers or documents. Engrossed in this task, she failed to hear the faint click of the front door opening again and soft, wary footsteps coming up behind her.

A heavy hand clamped around her upper arm, causing Jackie to let out a little scream of surprise and fear. Instinctively, she struggled to break free, but the vice-like grip held her firm. 'What do you think you're doing?' a gruff, male voice demanded.

Jackie whirled round, finally wrenching herself free. She stepped back quickly, sizing up the burly figure of the man who had accosted her. Physically powerful, he was a rough-looking figure, shabbily dressed, unshaven and with several teeth missing. His eyes had a wild, angry look in them. 'Who are you?' she asked uncertainly.

The man eyed her with suspicion. 'It's me who's asking the questions,' he muttered warily. 'I'm Joan's neighbour from the bungalow down the road. She asked me to keep an eye on the place while she was away. So, like I said – what do you think you're doing?'

Jackie started to relax, realising that the man did not pose a threat. 'I'm a police officer,' she told him, fishing for her ID card and producing it. 'Detective Constable Reid, Maryhill Police Station, Glasgow.'

'Ernie Watt,' the man said, 'I'm sorry, I thought you might be a burglar.'

Jackie smiled at him. 'It's all right,' she told him. 'Good neighbours like you make our job easier.' She paused, the smile fading from her face to be replaced by an expression of professional detachment. 'I don't know if you realise why I'm here, Mr Watt . . .' she started hesitantly, unsure whether he would have heard of Joan Mathieson's death.

The man nodded gravely. 'Aye, I heard the news,' he confirmed. 'I thought someone would come.' He shook his head slowly from side to side, sucking at his teeth. 'A terrible business,' he went on, sadly. 'She hated the city, you know. I drove her to the bus station. She was dreading going, even though she was excited about seeing her daughter, being there for the birth.' He paused again. 'It was as if she almost knew something was going to happen to her.'

'How well did you know her?' Jackie asked.

'Oh, thirty-odd years,' Watt answered, smiling faintly to himself at the memories. 'I knew the whole family – watched the children grow up. Lovely kids, they were.'

'She was a midwife, I believe?'

Watt nodded. 'Aye, and her mother before her. Maybe that's what made her so old-fashioned. Superstitious, she was.'

'In the twentieth century?' Jackie queried.

Watt grinned knowingly. 'Ah, the old superstitions, the country ways – they die hard. You know, Joan used to say that unbaptised babies turned into butterflies if they died.'

Jackie regarded him incredulously. 'And do you think she really *believed* that?'

Watt shrugged. 'Maybe she did, maybe she didn't. But I'll tell you one thing. She'd run a mile if one came near her. Like it really was the soul of a dead bairn.' The man pulled himself up suddenly, as if aware that he was prattling nonsense. 'Well, I'd best get about my business and leave you to yours. I'm just down the road if you need me.'

'Thanks,' Jackie told him. She watched him as Ernie Watt turned and sauntered away as quietly and softly as he had come. For such a big man, he moved with surprising stealth, Jackie reflected for a moment, before returning her attention to the bureau.

The wind was getting up as evening started to draw in. Jackie was tired already, and not looking forward to the drive back to Glasgow in the dark. But Taggart had instructed her to search the cottage thoroughly, and there was still one bedroom to go. Her efforts thus far had yielded little, apart from a bundle of shopping receipts which went back some four or five years and a couple of small insurance policies. There was virtually nothing in the way of personal correspondence and no sign of a will or any other type of legal document. Joan Mathieson's life, it appeared, had been simple, neat and very, very lonely.

Jackie addressed herself to the task again, sifting through the contents of the dead woman's wardrobe before moving on to the drawers of the bedside cabinet. In the bottom drawer, buried under a pile of neatly folded underwear, she finally came across a photo album. Jackie lifted it out, carrying it across to the bedside table and switching on the small table-lamp to study it more closely. Perhaps not surprisingly, the first dozen or so pages were filled with nothing but baby pictures. Jackie turned the pages slowly, progressing through a chronological portrait of a young family growing up, having birthdays, going to school. Then, suddenly, there was another oddity. As the children in the pictures grew towards their teenage years, gaps started to show up in the continuity. The pages of the album began to display more and more spaces where it was obvious that individual photographs had been deliberately removed, and in some cases roughly ripped out. Finally, there were more gaps than photos, and the record stopped completely.

Jackie closed the album, dropping it into a small suitcase which she had brought with her for the purpose. She found herself wondering, again, about the strange mind of Joan Mathieson. What kind of a woman, she mused, would go to the trouble of keeping a record of her children, then mutilate and destroy their pictures when they grew up?

Perhaps Taggart might make more sense of it, she thought. She searched through the remaining two drawers of the bedside cabinet and then closed the case, picking it up and getting ready to leave.

A faint knocking sound came to her ears, echoing down from the ceiling above her head. With a slight start, Jackie glanced upwards, trying to identify the sound and pinpoint its source. The sounds continued, an irregular pattern of dull yet positive blows like someone trying to tap out a morse-code message.

It was probably just the wind, Jackie thought. Nevertheless, she followed the source of the sound across the ceiling of the bedroom, reaching the door and stepping out on to the landing. She looked up again to see an attic hatch above her head which she had not noticed before.

It was definitely worth investigating. Jackie returned to the bedroom and dragged a wooden chair out on to the landing. Standing on it, she stretched up to try to reach the hatch. The tips of her fingers just failed to make contact. She jumped down from the chair, looking around for something which would give her the extra reach she needed. Her eyes fell on the small suitcase which she had laid down beside the chair. Picking it up, Jackie stepped up on to the chair again and held the case in both hands, pressing it against the edge of the hatch. There was a faint click as some sort of catch was released. Without warning, the hatch suddenly dropped open and a folding metal ladder began to descend rapidly towards her.

Caught by surprise, Jackie jumped backwards off

the chair with a sudden cry of alarm as the ladder crashed to the landing floor. She stared at it dumbly for a few moments, taking time to recover from her shock. Then curiosity took over. Taking a deep breath, Jackie mounted the first rungs of the ladder and began to clamber up into the gloomy attic.

There was a light switch just inside the rim of the hatchway. Jackie snapped it on, and the dim glow of a single naked 40-watt bulb lit up the interior of the surprisingly spacious attic. Jackie clambered in, looking around at a motley collection of dusty and cobweb-covered junk and debris which had accumulated over the years. There was an old-fashioned pram, various items of broken furniture, and a rocking crib. Jackie touched the crib, lightly, with her fingertips, setting it rocking gently with a faint squeak of old and rusted hinges.

The knocking sound came again. Jackie strained her eyes into the darkness beyond the glow of the light bulb, finally identifying a hole in the eaves where a tile had become loose. A dangling wooden slat flapped in the wind, tapping against the side of an abandoned bookshelf.

Jackie breathed a small sigh of relief, turning away and moving towards a large pile of junk on the left-hand side of the attic. There was a sudden screech of alarm and the frantic flapping of wings as a roosting pigeon rose into the air in front of her face. Jackie screamed instinctively, dropping to the floor and wrapping her arms above her head. The disturbed, frightened bird fluttered above her in panic for a few seconds then flew straight towards the hole in the eaves.

Jackie pulled herself together, feeling rather foolish. She clambered to her feet again, stepping over to the jumble of rubbish in the corner. Amongst the collection of old lampshades, broken children's toys and discarded magazines was a small wooden chest, about three feet long and perhaps eighteen inches deep. Jackie tested the lid experimentally. It was not locked. Folding the lid back, Jackie peered inside.

Nestling on top of some old baby clothes were a number of small, wrinkled objects all individually packaged in plastic food bags. Jackie pulled one out, holding it up towards the light. It appeared to be some sort of a membrane, perhaps made of latex or some soft plastic material. Her curiosity now fully aroused, Jackie slipped her fingers inside the bag, hooking the object out for a closer inspection.

A cold shiver ran through her as her fingertips made contact. Touch alone told her that it was not made of any synthetic material. With a feeling of revulsion, Jackie realised that what she was holding was a piece of dried skin – and the evidence of her eyes told her that it had not come from any animal she had ever seen. With another faint shudder, she thrust the object back inside its plastic covering and dropped it back into the chest. Three or four others which she pulled out were virtually identical – and each totally mystifying. Fascinated, Jackie rummaged deeper into the chest in search of further puzzles.

Soft footsteps padded through the ground floor of the cottage below her, but Jackie did not hear them. Nor did she hear the faint sound of liquid from a large can being splashed over curtains, carpeting and furniture. Perhaps the reek of evaporating petrol fumes might eventually have permeated the musty air of the attic to alert her, but they were not given a chance to do so. As the last dregs of the flammable liquid splashed out on to the staircase and banisters, the soft footsteps retreated.

Then there was only the momentary splutter of a struck match, and the dull whoosh of ignition as it was tossed on to the petrol-soaked floor of the cottage.

Jackie pulled an old and yellowing newspaper cutting from the very bottom of the chest. Unfolding it, she noticed that it was a front page story, taken from the *Western and Argyll Times*. The headline screamed out at her in 72-point bold: 'OBAN FISHING BOAT TRAGEDY'.

Further mystified by the question of why a woman who had lived her entire life in Perthshire should want to preserve a cutting from an Argyll newspaper, Jackie began to study the main text of the story, straining her eyes to read the small print in the poor light. It was almost impossible. Jackie edged closer to the single bulb and the mouth of the hatchway, where she could see a little more clearly. She wrinkled her nose delicately as the smell of burning reached her. She glanced towards the hatchway, just as the first tendrils of black, acrid smoke began to curl up into the attic.

She acted immediately, instinctively. Hastily grabbing a handful of the mysterious skin pieces out of the chest, she stuffed them into her pocket along with the newspaper cutting and snatched up the case containing the photo album and papers.

The black smoke was thick and choking now, swirling up in spiralling, convected clouds as the fire downstairs really took hold. Jackie coughed violently as she peered down through the top of the hatchway, just able to see the reddish glow of the licking, leaping flames through the smoky haze. Controlling the urge to panic, she ran back to the chest again and pulled out a handful of old baby clothes, pressing them over her nose and mouth as a makeshift smoke filter. Holding her breath,

TAGGART

she hurried back to the hatch opening and began to scramble down the ladder.

From the level of the landing, Jackie could see that there was no way past the fire to the ground floor. The hallway and the lower stairs were already a roaring mass of flames, long tongues of which were progressing, serpent-like, up the wooden banister rail. There was only one possible avenue of escape, and Jackie took it. She threw open the bedroom door, running into the room and dragging the sheets and coverlet from the neatly made bed. Hastily rolling them up, she closed the bedroom door firmly and threw the bedclothes to the floor, kicking them into the gap between the carpet and the bottom of the door with her shoes. It would suffice as a temporary smoke barrier, at least, she thought. She probably had several minutes before the actual heat and flames became a direct threat. Her priority at that moment was in getting some fresh air into her lungs. She ran across the bedroom to the window, throwing it open. Leaning out, she took several good, deep breaths to clear out the fumes she had already inhaled before sizing up her situation.

It was at least a sixteen-foot drop to the ground below, on to a small patch of lawn. Quickly, Jackie considered jumping straight away, then held herself in check, realising that she stood more than a fair chance of breaking both legs, if not her back. It was time for some good old-fashioned Girl Guides stuff, Jackie thought, with a flash of humour. She tossed the case out of the window and ran across to the bedside chest of drawers, remembering the stack of freshly ironed and folded bedsheets she had seen earlier. Pulling them out, she began to knot several together, corner to corner. Finally, having tested each join with a firm tug, she tied one end of the sheets securely round the leg of the bed and twisted them into a makeshift rope, which she carried to the window and dropped out. Heaving herself out over the windowsill, she clambered down her improvised fire escape to safety, dropping the last few feet on to the lawn and retreating quickly to the front gate.

Jackie looked back at the cottage, which was now a blazing inferno as the flames flew hungrily upon its old and well-dried wooden frame. Windows had already started to explode from the heat, and the first leaping tendrils of flame could now be seen appearing through the roof, turning the attic where she had been into a death-trap.

Pausing only for a matter of seconds to reflect on the narrowness of her escape, Jackie turned away from the blazing cottage and began to run down the country road towards Ernie Watt's bungalow.

There were lights on inside the bungalow, but no answer to her frantic knocking on the front door. After the third attempt, Jackie gave up, stepping back from the door and skirting around the front of the building. There was a wood and glass greenhouse built on to the side of the bungalow. It, too, was lit from inside. Jackie ran to it, pressing her face against the glass and peering in. Apart from rows of ripening tomato plants on long trestle tables and dozens of pots containing various seedlings and cuttings, there was no sign of life.

Jackie moved further along the side of the outhouse, finally coming to a half-glazed door. She tested the handle, then opened the door, stepping cautiously inside. 'Mr Watt?' she called out hopefully, but there was no answer.

She moved further inside, breathing heavily. Beyond the rows of tomato plants there was a half-partition, which partially screened off the greenhouse from the workroom area. As she approached it, Jackie could see that another one of the long trestle tables had been overturned, spilling its load on to the stone floor. Broken pieces of flowerpot scrunched beneath her feet as she walked.

She looked down at the ground, watching out for her step. Between the little mounds of earth and smashed pots, a thin, red river trickled stickily. With a growing tightness in her throat, Jackie took the last few steps to the partition and peered round it.

Ernie Watt was slumped on the floor like a discarded, life-sized puppet, his back propped up against the surface of the overturned table. The blood still flowed freely from a single, small, but deep puncture in his neck.

Chapter Eighteen

Recovered from her ordeal, Jackie Reid fought to see through the press of Taggart, Jardine and Superintendent McVitie as they crowded around the figure of Dr Andrews. He was examining the mysterious pieces of skin tissue which Jackie had found in Joan Mathieson's house, and which, up to now, had bemused and fascinated everybody in Maryhill Police Station. A man who was very possessive of his own, personal space, Andrews was more than a little irritated by the sheer number of people crowded around him, their faces all bearing much the same expression of morbid fascination.

'Well?' Taggart prompted him, impatiently. 'Is it human tissue?'

Andrews nodded. 'I would have thought that was

obvious – even to a layman,' he muttered, with unaccustomed sarcasm.

'So what are they?' Jackie asked, feeling that she somehow had the right to be the first to know, having discovered the objects.

'They're cauls,' Andrews said confidently. 'Part of the foetal membrane which sometimes clings to an infant's head at birth.'

'So where did they come from?' Jardine demanded.

Andrews looked up, treating him to an expression of pained indulgence. 'Probably from the heads of infants, I shouldn't wonder.'

Jardine fell silent, feeling well put in his place.

'Joan Mathieson was a midwife,' Jackie Reid put in. 'And her mother before her, it seems. That would explain how she came across these things – but why on earth would she want to collect them?' She broke off, remembering Ernie Watt's reference to Joan's superstitious nature. She pushed her way past Jardine, confronting Andrews directly. 'Dr Andrews – do you know of any old country lore or superstition attached to these things?'

Andrews nodded. 'There's almost inevitably some sort of fetishism attached to objects which symbolise birth – or death,' he pointed out. He poked one of the cauls with his forceps. 'In the case of these things, the most specific property was supposed to be in giving protection from drowning. Many sailors used to pay high prices for them. More generally, they were regarded as powerful talismans for good luck.'

McVitie grunted sceptically. 'They didn't bring Joan Mathieson much luck, did they?'

There was a curious look on Jackie Reid's face. Dr Andrews' reference to drowning sailors had turned up a puzzling, even slightly disturbing, connection. She pulled the newspaper cutting from her pocket, unfolding it and showing it to Taggart and Jardine.

'Then what do you think about this?' she asked. 'It was tucked away in the same chest, with the cauls.'

Taggart scanned the headline, his forehead creasing into a frown. Jackie was right – it *was* a strange coincidence. And Taggart didn't much care for coincidences. Finally, he nodded at her. 'You'd better check it out,' he muttered.

Jackie had not expected quite such an immediate reaction. She looked surprised. 'You want me to go to Oban now?'

Jardine could not resist a little joke. 'Only stay out of burning houses,' he warned her.

It was not appreciated, Jackie glared at him. 'I'll do my best.'

'You'll do better than that,' Taggart snapped at her, quite serious. He waved his finger in the air, to emphasise a point. 'And another thing – the next time your life's in danger, you don't stop to pick up evidence. You get out fast – is that understood?' He paused, his tone softening. 'I don't want your corpse on my hands as well.'

Jackie found his concern quite touching. She smiled sweetly. 'I sincerely hope the occasion won't arise again, sir,' she said, in what was a minor masterpiece of understatement. Taking the newspaper cutting back from Taggart's fingers, she ducked out of the crowd and headed towards the door.

Jardine had also noticed Taggart's obvious concern. He grinned broadly. 'So you do care for us, after all, sir?' he said facetiously.

Taggart glowered at him for a moment, then turned

his attention back to Dr Andrews. 'Now, if we could just get ourselves back to the business in hand,' he suggested, with heavy emphasis. 'What are your initial findings on the Ernie Watt killing?'

'Same weapon, Jim,' Andrews told him. 'A knitting needle, delivered to the same spot in the side of the neck. Virtually identical to the Mathieson murder. I'll leave the possible motive to you.'

'He was probably killed so he couldn't identify who set fire to the cottage,' Jardine put in. 'In an isolated spot like that, he'd probably notice every car that went past, any stranger within five miles. You know what country people are like.'

'But why?' McVitie queried. It was a scenario he couldn't quite understand. 'Why burn down the entire place? I can't believe that anyone would choose such a complicated, clumsy and hit-or-miss method to murder a police officer.'

Jardine shrugged. 'My gut feeling is that DC Reid wasn't the intended target at all,' he volunteered. 'Her presence could have been just an unfortunate coincidence. Perhaps the intention was just to destroy something which was in the cottage.'

'Or everything,' Taggart added, agreeing with Jardine's assessment. 'If that was the intention, it was certainly successful. The place was totally gutted.' He turned to Jardine. 'Find out exactly what Martin Adams was doing last night,' he instructed. 'In fact,' he added as an afterthought, 'you'd better check out the whole family while you're at it.'

McVitie had a few thoughts of his own. He pursed his lips, looking at Taggart with a slightly doubtful expression on his face. 'You are still sure that this is a domestic, Jim?'

'What else?' Taggart asked, with a shrug of his shoulders. 'But I'm open to any other suggestions.'

McVitie paused for a while. 'Well, for instance – could we perhaps be reading a bit more into the unusual choice of murder weapon?' he ventured hesitantly.

It took Taggart a few seconds to fall in with McVitie's chain of thought. When it finally clicked, he gave the idea scant consideration before shaking his head dismissively, a faint grin on his face. 'A woman, sir? I think you've been reading too many old Agatha Christie books.'

Chapter Nineteen

Cathy Adams opened the fridge door, bending down to take the orange juice from the cool shelf. The sudden contraction was not appreciated by the baby, who signalled his discomfort with a particularly strong kick. The feel of the tiny life stirring within her womb gave Cathy a little thrill of pleasure. She straightened up, slipping her hand under the baggy sweater she was wearing and stroking her abdomen tenderly as her unborn child made a few more squirming movements and then settled down again. She set the orange juice down on the breakfast table and waddled towards the conservatory.

Martin was hand-feeding a couple of butterflies with a sticky mixture of honey and peach juice. He looked up briefly as Cathy came in then returned his gaze to the delicate insects in his palm. Cathy sighed, sitting down beside him on the edge of the mud-pool. 'The baby's lively this morning,' she told him, proudly. 'I just felt him kick.'

Martin accepted the announcement without enthusiasm. He continued to gaze at his beloved butterflies, saying nothing.

'Would you like to feel him?' Cathy invited, standing up and pulling her sweater up to her navel. The offer was declined. Cathy sighed again, rolling her sweater down again. She was silent for a long while, staring at her husband with a hopeless mixture of love and sadness. 'Look, it doesn't really matter that he's Dr Millar's,' she murmured, finally. 'He's our baby – and that's what we always wanted. What *you* always said you wanted,' she added. She clutched at Martin's sleeve, causing the feeding butterflies to flutter away in alarm. 'Can't you try to love him, Martin?'

Martin let out a strange, choked little sound that was somewhere between a laugh and a sob. 'How can I?' he demanded bitterly. 'How can I even pretend he's mine, now? Everything's changed, everything's poisoned.'

'No!' Cathy shook her head violently, a pleading look in her eyes. 'It doesn't have to be like that, Martin. He'll be our child and you'll be his father, in every normal sense of the word.'

Martin turned towards her, grasping her by the shoulders in a firm grip. His eyes bored into hers coldly. 'Dr Millar is his father,' he said, flatly. 'And I'm never going to be able to forget that fact.'

Cathy's face was desperate. 'Then what's going to happen to us?' she asked in a frightened little voice. Her eyes filled with tears. 'What are we going to *do*, Martin?'

He dropped his hands from her shoulders, averting

his eyes from hers as though he was unable to face her with what he had to say. 'Look, I've been thinking about this a lot,' he said, after a long pause. 'And as I see it, there's only one thing we can do. We have him adopted and we try again – somewhere else.'

Cathy couldn't quite believe what she was hearing. Stunned and shocked, she fell back a couple of steps, staring blankly at the man who had suddenly become a complete stranger to her. Her wide-open eyes registered fear and confusion. 'You can't mean that,' she sobbed, incredulously.

'I'm sorry, Cathy. It's the only way,' Martin said gently. He stepped forwards to embrace her, help take away her pain.

Cathy moved away from him again, defiance beginning to blaze in her eyes. She clasped her hands across her swollen belly in a protective gesture. 'He's my baby,' she screamed at him. 'He's my baby, and I want him. And I'm going to keep him.'

Martin regarded her hopelessly for a few seconds, finally shrugging with resignation. 'Then you have him, Cathy,' he muttered coldly. He stepped past her on his way out of the conservatory. 'I'm going to work. Don't worry about breakfast. I'll grab a cup of coffee and a doughnut on my way to the office.'

After he had left the house, Cathy cried for a long time. She had only just started to pull herself together when the doorbell rang. Reluctantly, she answered it, to find Jardine standing on the doorstep, accompanied by a young WPC. Noticing her red-rimmed eyes, he was instantly apologetic. 'Look, I'm sorry if this is a bad time, Mrs Adams.'

Cathy shook her head slowly, ushering them both

in. 'No, it's all right. Every time's been a bad time for the past few days.'

Jardine nodded understandingly, following her into the living-room. He waited until she had seated herself before starting. 'I'm sorry to have to tell you, Cathy – but your mother's cottage was burned to the ground last night.' He did not mention the murder of Ernie Watts. It was perhaps best if she didn't know at that point.

Only a vague look of surprise showed in Cathy's eyes. It was as if she was beyond shock, Jardine thought. So traumatised by the events of the last few days that nothing could quite get through to her anymore.

'I'm sorry I have to ask you this – but where was your husband last night between seven and ten o'clock?' he went on.

Cathy answered without hesitation. 'He was home with me, all evening.'

Jardine smiled at her gently. 'Now you wouldn't be covering up for him, would you, Mrs Adams?'

Cathy regarded him with wide-eyed innocence. She seemed genuinely surprised at the question. 'Why would I want to do that?'

Jardine shrugged. 'Wives sometimes do,' he muttered.

Cathy nodded understandingly. 'Yes, of course. Well, if I had to cover up for Martin, perhaps I would,' she said honestly. 'But in this case I don't. As I told you, he was here with me from six o'clock when he got home from work.'

It was the end of that particular line of questioning, Jardine realised. He fished in his pocket, drawing out the newspaper cutting which Jackie had found in Joan Mathieson's house. He showed it to Cathy. 'Do you have any idea why your mother might have kept this?' he asked.

Cathy took the cutting and scanned it briefly, a puzzled look coming into her eyes. She handed it back to him, shaking her head. 'I haven't the faintest idea,' she told him.

'It was in an old chest, in the attic,' Jardine said, producing one of the cauls. 'Along with a number of these.'

A thin but knowing smile showed briefly on Cathy's face. She stood up, moving across the room to open a wall-safe, concealed behind a piece of modern art. When she returned, she was holding an identical piece of dried tissue in her hand. 'Snap,' she said, showing it to Jardine. He regarded her quizzically. Cathy answered the unspoken question. 'Mum said I was born with it. She told me it would bring me luck.' She broke off to laugh bitterly. 'Fat lot of luck, eh?'

Jardine glanced down at her distended belly. 'How long before the baby's due?' he enquired.

Just for a brief instant, the faintest trace of happiness flickered on Cathy's face. 'Three weeks, two days – and about fifteen minutes.' The smile faded. 'Are you a father?' she asked, curiously.

Jardine shook his head. 'I'm not even married.'

It didn't seem to matter, from Cathy's point of view. He was a man. Another young man. 'What would you do – if you were Martin?' she asked him suddenly.

Put on the spot, Jardine could only answer her in all honesty. 'I don't know,' he said simply.

It wasn't good enough. 'Could you learn to love another man's child?' Cathy went on. She stared at Jardine intently as he squirmed with embarrassment. For her, the answer was written on his face.

'You couldn't – could you?' she said miserably. It was a statement rather than a question. She stared across the room at the pram. 'Mum said it was unlucky to bring a pram into the house before the baby was born. Maybe she was right in some things, after all.'

Dr Millar was loading fishing tackle and keep nets into a small rowing skiff as his wife drove up to the lochside cottage. He looked up, watching her as she climbed out of the car with a bag of groceries under her arm and strolled down to the small jetty to join him.

'I didn't know if you'd be coming today,' Millar muttered. 'I was just going out to do a spot of fishing to pass the time.'

Ruth delved into the carrier bag she was carrying, bringing out a packet of tobacco and a newspaper. 'I brought you some pipe tobacco,' she murmured.

'Thanks,' Millar said, taking it and slipping it into his pocket. 'That was thoughtful of you.'

'And this,' Ruth added, thrusting the newspaper into his hands.

Millar glanced at the headline: 'CLINIC DOCTOR COULD FACE MULTIPLE FRAUD CHARGES'. He looked up at his wife with a faint shrug. 'It doesn't matter. I heard the news on the radio this morning. It's still not definite. They're not even sure yet whether they can make the charges stick.'

'I also brought some fish for lunch,' Ruth announced.

Millar flashed her a short, rueful smile. 'Have you really abandoned all faith in me?' he asked.

Ruth didn't answer him, merely turning her back and walking away up to the cottage.

Chapter Twenty

Jackie Reid drove down the winding hill to the harbour-side and along the promenade, past the tiny inner harbour with its collection of small fishing and day boats.

As its name suggested, Harbourview Terrace was a short, curving row of houses which was built just beyond the inner harbour. 'Seahorses' was the corner house, with a long front garden which stretched all the way down to the rocky beach below. Jackie pulled up outside it and climbed out of the car, walking up to the tousle-haired young man who was working on the engine of a motorcycle by the side of the house. He looked up at her with a rather vacant expression on his face as she approached. He seemed a bit on the dim-witted side, Jackie thought. She smiled at him gently, trying to put him at his ease. 'Does Mrs Moore live here?' Jackie enquired.

The young man seemed to have to think about it, finally nodding. 'That's my Mum,' he announced, as though he had only just figured it out. He returned to tinkering with the motorbike.

'Well, is she in?' Jackie asked, after a while.

The young man shook his head, dumbly. He did not attempt to volunteer any further information.

Jackie made a conscious effort to avoid her growing irritation from showing in her voice. 'Could you tell me when she's likely to be back?' she enquired as gently as possible. 'It's important that I talk to her.'

The word 'important' appeared to get through. The young man stood up, nodding down the length of the garden towards a figure on the shingle below. 'She's down on the beach,' he announced.

'Thanks,' Jackie muttered, unable to keep a hint of sarcasm from her tone. She began to walk down the garden towards the woman on the beach, who was collecting seaweed in a bucket.

The woman straightened, regarding Jackie somewhat warily as she approached. Aware that Jackie was looking at the bucket of seaweed with a rather puzzled expression, she ventured an explanation. 'It's for the garden. Better than any compost you can buy.'

'Oh!' Jackie muttered, nodding understandingly. It was a piece of useful information that life in Glasgow had never furnished before. She paused for a moment. 'Mrs Moore? I'd like a few words with you.'

The woman looked quite surprised that anyone should want to talk to her. 'What about?' she said guardedly.

Jackie produced her ID. 'I'm Detective Constable

Jackie Reid, from Glasgow. I'm investigating the murder of a Mrs Joan Mathieson,' she said.

Mrs Moore's eyes flickered uncertainly. 'What's that got to do with me?' she demanded – a trifle *too* aggressively, Jackie thought.

'She had an old newspaper cutting in her possession,' Jackie went on. She produced a photostat of the clipping from her pocket. 'I'd like you to take a look at it, if you wouldn't mind.'

Jackie handed the woman the cutting, unable to miss the fact that her hands were trembling quite noticeably as she reached out to accept it. Mrs Moore stared at the headline, and the rather grainy picture of the heavily-bearded young man below it. She gave a little sob. 'Oh my God,' she muttered, shuddering.

'He was your husband, wasn't he?' Jackie asked, gently.

Mrs Moore nodded, folding the cutting and handing it back. She was silent for a long time, and when she finally spoke there was a nervous catch in her voice. 'That was over twenty years ago. Why do you have to come here stirring it all up again now?'

Jackie was apologetic. 'I'm sorry if it's painful for you. But, as I said – we're interested as to why Mrs Mathieson would have kept this cutting. Did you know her?'

Mrs Moore shook her head. 'I've never heard of her.'

Jackie was not convinced. 'Would you like me to repeat the name? Joan Mathieson. She lived in the village of Afford in Perthshire.'

'She could have lived in Balmoral Castle,' Mrs Moore snapped back at her. 'I told you – I've never heard of her.'

The woman was lying, Jackie was certain. Her very aggression was a form of defence, an indication that she was hiding something. But how to force an admission? Jackie tried another tack. 'Perhaps your son has heard of her?' she suggested.

Mrs Moore snorted derisively. 'It'd be no good asking him anything. He's the thickest of the lot. He wouldn't have heard of Robert the Bruce.'

'How many children do you have?' Jackie asked, more to keep a conversation going than anything else. If she could keep the woman talking, there was always the possibility that she could gain her confidence, draw her out.

'Five,' Mrs Moore answered. She nodded her head up towards her son. 'But none of them live at home except Roy. I'll probably be stuck with him for life.' She looked at Jackie with a tired expression. 'Look, you're wasting your time, Miss. I don't know this woman you're talking about, and I haven't got the faintest idea why she might have kept this cutting. Some people just collect clips from old newspapers.'

It was not a satisfactory explanation. Jackie shook her head. 'This wasn't part of a collection. It was on its own – as though it was important to her in some way.' She produced one of the cauls from her pocket. 'Did your husband own one of these?'

Mrs Moore regarded the object with a look of faint disgust, wrinkling her nose. 'What the hell is that?'

'It's a caul,' Jackie explained. 'Part of the foetal membrane of a newly born infant.'

Mrs Moore regarded Jackie as though she was some sort of an idiot. 'Now why on earth would my husband keep something like that?' she demanded.

Jackie shrugged. 'I'm told lots of sailors kept them as talismans – lucky charms,' she said.

Mrs Moore let out a short, bitter and dismissive snort. 'Ronnie wasn't a sailor. He just liked messing about in boats, when his work at the hospital let him.' She paused, sighing. 'He wasn't even a particularly strong swimmer, poor devil.'

It looked as though there was nothing more to be gained from prolonging the interview, Jackie thought. She pulled a card from her pocket and scribbled on it, handing it to the woman. 'Look, there's my name and number,' she said. 'Give me a call if you think of anything which might help us.' Jackie turned away to walk back up the garden. A sudden flash of light from the direction of the house caught her attention, and she squinted her eyes, peering up at it.

Roy Moore was watching them both through an old-fashioned brass ship's telescope. Suddenly aware that he had been spotted, he hastily folded it up, dropped it to the ground and went back to fiddling with his motorbike.

Chapter Twenty-one

Tom Fleming manoeuvred the shredding machine trailer into the garage, backing it up to his workbench before unhitching it from the Land Rover. Returning to the machine, he began to unscrew the safety plate covering the shredder blades. Ian watched his uncle morosely, glancing at his watch. It was tea-time, and he was hungry. 'Do you have to do that now?'

Tom glanced up, nodding. 'She's been playing up all day. I think the blades need cleaning. We've got too much tied up in this new contract to risk it packing up on us tomorrow.' He dug into the pocket of his overall, pulling out a £10 note and waving it in Ian's direction. 'Look, why don't you go down to the pub and have a beer, then pop into the chippie and bring us back some supper? I only need about three-quarters of an hour.'

Ian accepted the offer quickly, before his uncle had a chance to change his mind. He stepped across, taking the note. 'Cod and mushy peas? Or would you like a nice piece of skate for a change?'

'Aye, cod will be fine,' Tom muttered. He turned back to the shredder as Ian left. Confident that he had just bought himself a good uninterrupted hour, he smiled to himself as he unscrewed the safety plate and lowered it to the floor. As he had expected, the shredder blades were badly fouled up, but there was another problem. A couple of particularly green and sinewy saplings had managed to get themselves twined around the drive-shaft and would need cutting out. Tom stood up, turning round to his workbench to get a small hacksaw, and was surprised to see Ian standing there by the garage door.

'That was quick,' Tom started to joke, then noticed the grim look on his nephew's face.

'We've got a visitor,' the lad announced gravely, stepping aside to let Cathy in. Her face was drawn and strained, and she looked on the verge of tears.

Tom wiped his hands hurriedly on the front of his overall, stepping forward to grasp her by the shoulders. 'Cathy, love – whatever's wrong?' he enquired, with genuine concern in his voice.

The tears broke. Cathy laid her head against her uncle's chest, sobbing pitifully. 'It's Martin,' she managed to blurt out. 'He says he doesn't want us to keep the baby. He wants to have it adopted.'

Behind her, Ian exploded angrily. 'He said *what*?' he demanded. 'I'll kill him.' He broke off awkwardly, aware that his reaction was a trifle hasty and over the top. After a few seconds, he appeared to simmer down, modifying his response. 'I'll go round and talk some sense into

160

him,' he muttered. 'If necessary, I'll *knock* some sense into him.'

Tom glared at him over Cathy's shoulder. 'You'll do no such thing,' he snapped. He looked down at Cathy's tearful face. 'Come on, we'll go and have a nice cup of tea and talk about it calmly and quietly,' he murmured in a gentle voice. Slipping a paternal arm around her shoulders, he led her towards the house.

'Now, what exactly did Martin say?' Tom prompted, after he had sat Cathy down and despatched Ian to make the tea.

Cathy was calmer now, although still very upset. She gave her uncle a brief account of her conversation with her husband. When she had finished, she looked up at him with a desperate, pleading look in her eyes. 'I can't give up my baby, Uncle – I just can't.'

Tom patted her hand reassuringly. 'Nobody's going to force you to do that, Cathy,' he assured her. 'Ian and I are your family now, and we're not going to let anything or anybody make you do anything you don't want to.'

Ian came into the room with the tea at that precise moment. 'I still think I ought to go round and have it out with him,' he muttered.

Tom was adamant. 'There's been enough bad blood in this family already,' he said heavily. 'That's what half of Cathy's troubles are about. There's no sense in any more harm being done.' He turned back to his niece. 'You tried for years,' he reminded her. 'And Martin agreed to choosing this way to have a baby. He has no right to tell you to have it adopted – no right at all.'

'And anyway – we'll all help you look after him,' Ian put in, trying to be helpful.

Instead, the suggestion seemed to upset Cathy afresh. Tears pricked out in her eyes again. 'I don't want to have to choose between them, I couldn't bear that,' she said miserably.

'Then don't even think about it,' Tom told her gently. 'You've just got to make sure the baby feels loved. They can tell, even inside there. And then, when he's born and Martin sees the way you feel – well, maybe he'll feel different too.'

Cathy was unconvinced. She shook her head sadly. 'He won't, I know he won't. Dr Millar said that babies born by donor insemination can sometimes become levers in domestic battles.'

'That bastard should know,' Ian spat out, finding another target to vent his anger on. Tom silenced him with a warning glare.

'If you have him adopted, you'll never forgive Martin,' he said to Cathy, spelling it out as simply as he saw it. 'It'll destroy you, and it'll destroy your marriage. Do you want to lose both of them?'

Cathy sniffed back her tears, shaking her head.

'Well, then,' Tom went on. 'You've just got to stick up for yourself, Cathy – make Martin see that you're not going to be bullied into a rash decision. Maybe Dr Millar is the baby's father – but you're his mother, Cathy. You're the one who's carried him all this time, and you're the one who has to make any decisions that need to be made.'

It was sound, old-fashioned advice that made good sense, Cathy realised. She wiped away the last of her tears with the back of her hand, forcing a brave smile. 'I think I'll have that cup of tea now,' she murmured.

*

Ruth Millar was boxing up some pieces of medical equipment in the clinic when Taggart strolled in. She looked up in surprise, not aware that she had left the front door on the latch. 'I'm sorry, but the clinic is closed,' she told him.

Taggart looked a trifle sheepish, embarrassed at having been mistaken for a putative father. He pulled out his ID card and introduced himself. 'Must have been quite an ordeal for you,' he muttered finally.

Ruth allowed herself a wry grin. 'You're quite a believer in understatements, Mr Taggart.'

'Have you had any more trouble?' Taggart asked.

Ruth shook her head. 'Not since we moved, but I'm sure it's only a matter of time. No doubt there will be another wave of righteous indignation once the trial starts.'

'You must have a very forgiving nature,' Taggart observed.

Ruth eyed him coolly. 'I think you must have misunderstood me. I said nothing of the sort,' she said firmly. 'Anyway, what did you want to see me about?'

'Joan Mathieson,' Taggart said. 'You met her at the christening of Rob Gibson's baby, I believe?'

Ruth nodded, but looked slightly puzzled. 'Only very briefly,' she pointed out. 'We were introduced, that was all.'

'And how did she seem to you? I mean, what sort of a mental state was she in?'

Ruth considered for a few seconds, remembering how Cathy's mother had refused to shake her hand. 'Nervous, even a bit strange,' she told Taggart finally. 'But then Cathy told her who I was, and I put it down to that.' She paused to smile thinly. 'Some older people still tend to regard artificial insemination as some kind of sacrilege – tinkering with the laws of nature.'

Taggart had to repress a quiet grin. 'Tinkering with the law' certainly applied in Colin Millar's case. 'Did you go to every christening?' he asked.

Ruth shook her head. 'No – although my husband did.'

Taggart caught her eyes in a direct confrontation. 'Then why did you go to this one, particularly?' he wanted to know.

Ruth returned his gaze with a cool, level stare. 'Because Cathy asked me to,' she said simply. 'She wanted us both to meet her mother, perhaps put her at her ease. As it happened, we didn't get the chance. The woman obviously didn't want to talk to me, and Colin was late arriving.'

Taggart nodded thoughtfully. Ruth Millar's answer sounded plausible enough, if in slightly dubious taste. 'Did you not think that it was a wee bit tactless?' he asked. 'Both of you turning up at a christening?'

'Tactless? How?' Ruth demanded, countering the suggestion. 'No one else would have known who we were. There were several babies being christened that day. Besides, parents that we've helped in the past have often wanted us there, discreetly in the background.'

Again, it seemed a reasonable answer. 'But your husband, of course, had his own reasons?' Taggart pointed out.

Ruth shot him a chilling glance. 'Is there anything else?' she demanded. 'I really need to get this equipment packed up safely.'

'Just one thing,' Taggart said. 'Did you see Joan Mathieson when she ran out of the church?'

Ruth nodded. 'Yes. We were sitting at the other end of the same row.'

'And as a medical person – I suppose a phobia would explain behaviour like that?'

Ruth looked slightly irritated by this new line of questioning. 'Look, I'm not a psychiatrist,' she pointed out. She paused, relenting slightly. 'But yes, I suppose phobias can make people do seemingly irrational things.'

Taggart was silent for a while, digesting this. 'Where would such a strange phobia come from – about butter-flies?' he asked finally.

It was the final straw for Ruth. She returned to the packing cases and resumed the work which Taggart had interrupted. 'All our deepest fears start in one place,' she muttered over her shoulder. 'In childhood.'

Chapter Twenty-two

The light was getting bad. Cursing under his breath, Tom Fleming straightened up from bending over the shredder and crossed to his workbench, plugging in an inspection lamp which he carried back to the machine. He glanced at his watch anxiously, aware that time was running short. It was already past nine o'clock and the shredder was still not running properly. It would have to be in top-notch order to cope with the next day's workload, and he needed a good night's sleep. At the moment, the way things were going, the two things were seeming increasingly incompatible.

Much as he cared for his niece, Cathy's visit could not have come at a more inconvenient time, he thought regretfully. It had taken a good two hours to calm her sufficiently to let her go home, and his own estimate of the time it would take to fix the shredder had proved woefully inadequate. The problem was a bit more complicated than just fouled blades, and the machine was obviously in need of a major overhaul – for which Tom had neither the time nor the expertise. The best he could hope for was to patch it up for another few days.

He made a couple more adjustments to the main drive-shaft coupling and stood up again, starting the machine for yet another test run. The powerful motor coughed noisily into life, spluttered a few times and then built up to a steady, throbbing roar. Engaging the shredding gear, Tom stepped back, his head cocked slightly to one side as he listened to the sound of it.

It still sounded lumpy, and there was a lot more vibration than he would have liked, but the machine appeared to be operating more or less normally, Tom thought. But the proof of the pudding was in the eating. He looked around the garage for something to stuff into the feeder hopper. Nothing really suitable came to his eye immediately. There was a pile of old cardboard boxes in one corner of the workshop, but they wouldn't present the whirling blades with any real challenge. Tom also rejected a bundle of rather heavy lumber on the opposite grounds. He thought for a few moments, finally remembering that Ian had left a load of scrub and garden waste in the trailer out in the yard. Dropping his tools to the floor, he walked to the door, opening it and kicking a can of herbicide into place to keep it ajar.

He walked across to the trailer, leaning over it and scooping up a load of twigs and branches between his arms. Holding the bundle tightly to his chest, he turned back towards the garage, freezing in his tracks momentarily as he noticed that the workshop door was now closed again.

His initial, faint prickle of alarm was swamped almost immediately by the instinctive tendency to rationalise anything unusual. It was probably the wind which had blown the door shut, Tom thought to himself, neglecting the fact that there was only the faintest breeze in the air. Shrugging to himself, he carried his load back across the yard and turned, pushing the door open again with his behind and preparing to ease through it backwards with his unwieldy burden.

The noise of the shredder was deafening, drowning out the faint sounds of movement behind the door as the figure lurking behind it stepped back out of the way. Tom backed over the threshold, turning towards the throbbing machine.

His body jerked and stiffened suddenly, as the thin blade of a steel knitting needle was plunged into the side of his neck. Tom's arms flew open, the bundle of twigs and branches spewing out under his feet as he staggered forward.

Half-blinded with pain and choking on his own blood, Tom Fleming was powerless to resist as he felt hands clamp themselves around his shoulders, propelling his sagging body across the workshop floor towards the roaring, grating shredder. He was only dimly aware of his hips being slammed heavily against its metal sides, of his body being arched over, his head being pushed down into the gaping maw of the feeder. But somehow, through it all, the full horror of his fate managed to get through to his befuddled brain.

Just before the wicked, whirling blades crunched into bone and flesh, screaming out with mechanical resistance against the clogging, gristly load they had never been designed to cope with, Tom Fleming screamed. The tortured squeal of metal, and the heavy throbbing of the motor, drowned out this final and bloodcurdling horror.

The noise of the machine rose to a crescendo, the walls of the garage and workshop picking up the erratic vibrations of the labouring machine to echo and amplify the din. With one last shriek of machinery pushed beyond its limit, the shredder blades floundered on their sticky, cloying meal and seized up. The motor coughed, spluttered, and stalled.

Then there was only a terrible and final silence.

Nobody should have to start their day like this, Dr Andrews thought, with a faint shudder. He'd been smiling as he walked across to the garage in the early morning sunlight. He was smiling no longer, as he stared at the thick gouts of red, lumpy goo splattered across the wall.

Jardine glanced at the man's pale and shaken face, noting the expression of utter disgust. 'So – there are still even things which turn your stomach,' he muttered, surprised. 'Well, if you don't mind, I'll leave this one to you.'

Andrews made no reply as Jardine turned away and headed for the open door, pausing outside for just long enough to take in a slow, deep breath of fresh air. Feeling a little better for it, he strode over to where Jackie Reid was standing protectively over the figure of Ian Mathieson, slumped down on the front doorstep of the house. The lad looked utterly shell-shocked, Jardine thought.

'I'm sorry,' Jardine muttered, knowing that anything he could say would be totally inadequate. He paused for a few moments of respectful silence. 'When did you find him?' he asked eventually.

Ian answered without looking up. 'First thing this morning. When I came out to hitch up the trailer.'

Jardine nodded. 'And when did you see him last?'

'About eight o'clock last night,' Ian answered. 'I went down to the pub.'

'Alone?' Jackie Reid asked.

Ian nodded. 'Uncle Tom was going to be working late on the shredder. It was playing up, and we had a lot of work to get through today.'

'Weren't you surprised when you came home and found he was not in the house?' Jardine wanted to know.

Ian shrugged hopelessly. 'I didn't think about it. I came back quite late, and I assumed he'd gone to bed early. He often did.'

'Why didn't you stay to help him with the shredder?' Jardine asked. 'If it was so important to your work?'

'Uncle Tom wouldn't have wanted me to. He says ... he said, I wasn't very good with mechanical things.' Ian finally looked up, a slightly troubled expression on his face. 'You make it sound as though I let him down, leaving him on his own like that.'

'We didn't say that, Ian,' Jackie reassured him, sympathising with the young man's misplaced sense of guilt.

Jardine, not so sensitive, saw only the possibility of something hidden. 'Did anything happen between you and your uncle last night?' he wanted to know.

Ian shook his head vehemently. 'Of course not.'

'Are you sure?' Jardine pushed the issue, convinced that the lad was holding something back. Catching Jardine's penetrating gaze, Ian looked slightly flustered. 'There *was* something, wasn't there?' Jardine prompted.

Ian finally shrugged. 'Just Cathy coming round,' he

admitted. 'Uncle Tom was worried that I was going to have a row with Martin because she was so upset.'

This sounded interesting, Jardine thought. 'So why did Cathy come round here?' he demanded.

'Just to talk. I told you – she was upset.'

'Upset about what, exactly?' Jardine had the fish on the hook now, and he wasn't going to let it off.

Ian looked increasingly uncomfortable, as though he had strayed into things best left alone. 'The baby,' he muttered evasively, but Jardine was on him like a flash.

'What about the baby?'

Ian sighed, realising that he was going to have to tell the full story. 'Martin had told her he didn't want the baby. He suggested that they have it adopted,' he said. 'Cathy was frightened and confused. She didn't know what to do, so she came to Uncle Tom for advice.'

'And what advice did he give her?'

Ian lowered his eyes to the ground, his voice dropping to a mere whisper. 'He told her that if it came to a choice between Martin and the baby, then she should keep the baby,' he admitted.

There was a slightly triumphant look on Jardine's face, as a couple more of the puzzle pieces clicked together. 'And I suppose it's a reasonable bet that your sister would have gone straight home and told Martin exactly what your uncle had said,' he suggested.

Ian nodded miserably, knowing that he had finally given Jardine what he wanted. 'Cathy never could keep a problem to herself,' he muttered.

Nodding thoughtfully to himself, Jardine glanced across at Jackie Reid, an unspoken question in his eyes. She could only give him a faint shrug of acquiescence. As circumstantial evidence went, it was more than enough.

Chapter Twenty-three

For the second time in five years, Taggart was surprised to find Peter Livingstone standing on his doorstep, looking uncharacteristically sheepish. This time, however, he was less effusive about his welcome. He eyed the young man warily. 'You'd better come in,' Taggart grunted. 'I was just having my breakfast.' He led the way into the kitchen and seated himself back at the table, buttering a fresh slice of toast. He nodded at the teapot on the table. 'Pour yourself a cup of tea if you'd like one.'

'Thanks.' Livingstone sat down opposite and helped himself. He said nothing as Taggart nibbled at his toast, more than a little edgy. It was a very strained atmosphere.

Finally, Taggart spoke. 'You put me in a very compromising position, Peter,' he muttered. It was as much a complaint as an accusation.

Livingstone looked suitably chastened. He hung his head abjectly. 'Yes, I know. I'm sorry,' he said simply.

There was another long and awkward silence, again eventually broken by Taggart. 'Well, what am I supposed to do?' he demanded, as though appealing for help. 'I can't get charges dropped just because you used to be a partner of mine. Or because I'm going to be your kid's godfather.'

Livingstone looked at him across the table. He seemed surprised that Taggart should even be considering such a thing. 'I know that, Jim – and I wouldn't expect you to,' he said firmly. 'That's not why I'm here.' He paused for a moment, sipping at his tea. 'Look, Jim – the reason I called round is to say that I know I compromised you, and that I'm sorry. But the point is – are you still willing to be Xavier's godfather?'

Now it was Taggart's turn to look surprised. 'Of course I am,' he said.

Livingstone nodded. 'Good. Because I want you to be.'

The tension in the room was starting to evaporate. Taggart grinned wryly. 'What – even when I'm an overbearing bully?' he queried.

Livingstone flashed the man a slightly rueful, apologetic smile. 'I was rather emotional,' he muttered.

'And perhaps truthful?' Taggart suggested.

Livingstone pushed his cup further across the table, using the space to rest his elbows and forming his hands into a bridge to rest his chin on. He stared directly into Taggart's eyes. It was almost a challenge. 'Look, Jim – I'd like you to try and understand why I did what I did. I think you'd have done something very much the same, under similar circumstances. Maybe even gone further than me.'

Taggart nodded slowly. 'Aye – very possibly,' he conceded. He crunched at his toast reflectively.

'A lot of people have said Xavier looks like me,' Livingstone murmured, suddenly. 'So at least I've got that.' He broke off, frowning slightly. 'Though he'll have to know the truth, one day, when he's old enough.'

The kitchen door swung open at that point, as Jean wheeled herself into the room. She caught the expression on Livingstone's face and froze, looking almost embarrassed. Taggart noticed his wife's concern, and smiled at her. 'It's all right, Jean – we're still going to be godparents,' he announced.

Livingstone forced a smile too. 'Marta and I have arranged to have him christened this evening,' he told Jean. 'I hope that's not too short notice for you?'

'Why the great urgency?' Taggart asked, a little insensitively.

Livingstone looked slightly awkward. 'Well, you know – under the circumstances,' he muttered hesitantly. 'The truth is, we've decided to get away for a month or so, until this Millar business is over. We thought we'd pay an extended visit to Marta's parents.'

Jean cut his explanation short, speaking for both of them. 'Under the circumstances, Peter – we'd be delighted,' she said confidently. She smiled sweetly at her husband. 'Isn't that right, Jim?'

Caught on the hop, Taggart could only nod in agreement. 'Oh – aye,' he muttered, none too convincingly.

The telephone rang, rescuing him. Taggart strode across the room, snatching it up. 'Taggart here. What is it?'

It was Jardine. Very quickly, he outlined the basic facts of Tom Fleming's murder, and his interview with Ian.

'So I think it's time we had another little talk with Martin Adams, sir,' he concluded.

Taggart nodded grimly. 'Aye – bring him in,' he snapped. 'I'm on my way.'

Martin Adams was standing by the mud pool in the conservatory observing a pair of colourful swallowtail butterflies as Jardine and Jackie Reid walked in. Although aware of their presence, he ignored them for a long time before finally speaking without looking round. 'Beautiful, aren't they?' he murmured absently. 'Sometimes, when the world seems ugly, I come in here just to forget about things.'

He turned, slowly, to face them directly at last. Jardine's face was set in a grim mask. 'Right now it's very ugly indeed, Martin,' he said flatly.

Adams nodded, as though he understood. He moved reluctantly away from the mud pool. 'I'll just get my coat,' he said.

Taggart and McVitie both faced Adams squarely across the desk in Interview Room 2. 'So you admit that you went round to Tom Fleming's house last night?' Taggart said, recapping on their previous conversation.

Adams nodded. 'I told you – I went round to have it out with him, tell him to keep his nose out of my private affairs. I rang the doorbell, but there was no answer, so I left again. I did not go anywhere near the garage.'

'It's all quite a coincidence, isn't it?' McVitie observed pointedly. 'You have a row with your mother-in-law and she dies violently. You go with the admitted purpose of having another row with your wife's uncle, and he dies even more violently.'

Adams glowered at him. 'I didn't go to have a row, I went to talk,' he corrected. 'And anyway, I'm not a violent person,' he added.

'That's hardly borne out by the evidence,' Taggart pointed out sceptically.

Adams was almost scornful. 'What evidence?'

'Your part in the assault on Dr Millar,' Taggart said quietly.

Just the mention of the man's name seemed to incense Adams. He thumped the desk angrily with his fist, glaring at Taggart. 'Dammit – I was doing what any father would have done. What you'd have done yourself.' He glanced at McVitie. 'And what you might have done, if you were younger.' The reference to his age was not appreciated. McVitie gave the young man a black look. Adams simmered down. 'Look, you won't make me admit to something I didn't do,' he stated flatly. 'Think about it – I'd hardly admit that I went round there with the intention of an argument if I'd killed him, would I?'

It was a good point, and one which had been worrying Taggart, but he didn't allow his feelings to show. 'Where did you go after you left the Fleming house?' he demanded.

Adams answered without hesitation. 'I called on Rob Gibson – the copper you suspended for taking part in the assault.'

'What time?' Taggart asked.

Adams shrugged. 'Around nine o'clock,' he said, a

little vaguely. 'But it was exactly ten when I left, because the late news had just come on the telly.'

'And DC Gibson will confirm this?' McVitie put in.

Adams nodded his head emphatically. 'His wife Michelle was there too. They'll both tell you I wasn't covered in blood – or covered in anything.'

It was another – extremely crucial – point. Taggart and McVitie exchanged a brief, dubious glance. Things weren't looking at all promising.

McVitie's surreptitious nod gave Taggart the answer he was seeking – and the one he had been expecting. He nodded over to the uniformed officer standing by the interview room door. 'Take Mr Adams down to a holding cell, will you,' he muttered.

Adams made no protest as the officer stepped over to escort him away. There didn't seem much point. After he had been taken away, Taggart looked at McVitie, sighing deeply. 'I think he's telling the truth, sir,' he muttered. 'I don't think he killed anyone.'

McVitie raised one querulous eyebrow. 'Are you getting mellow, Jim?' he asked. 'I remember the time when you'd have hammered him to the wall.'

Taggart grinned. 'I fancy you'd have liked to do that yourself, sir.'

McVitie nodded, a wry smile on his face. 'Aye – and I'm not too old to have done it, either.' His face was suddenly businesslike again. 'Seriously, Jim – can we afford to let Adams off the hook quite so easily? In both instances, he had the motive, he had the opportunity – and he most certainly has the temper.'

Taggart nodded, conceding both points. 'But he had no reason for burning down Joan Mathieson's house,' he pointed out. 'Or murdering her neighbour.'

Chapter Twenty-four

Jardine was studying the photographs of all the Millar children on the notice-board as Jackie strolled into the office. Noticing her, he waved a slip of paper in the air to attract her attention. 'I took a telephone message for you, about ten minutes ago,' he told her as she came over to join him. 'It was from Mrs Moore – the woman you went to see in Oban. She wants to see you again.'

Jackie regarded him with a curious expression on her face. 'Did she say what about?'

Jardine shook his head. 'Wouldn't discuss it with me at all. Said it had to be you – in person.'

Jackie nodded thoughtfully. 'I knew she wasn't telling me everything,' she mused. 'I just *knew* it.' She glanced at her watch. 'Well, I suppose I'd better get up there.' She looked up at Jardine. 'Fancy coming along with me, for the company?'

'Sure.' Jardine was glad of a chance to get out of the office. 'In fact, we'll take my car, if you like.'

'Why not?' Jackie shrugged, turning to follow him out to the car park.

There was something big going on at Mrs Moore's house as they arrived. Three police cars were parked in the road outside, and there were uniformed officers swarming all over the garden. Jackie jumped out of the car, closely followed by Jardine. Ducking under the police tapes which had been erected, they hurried towards the front of the house just as two officers were bringing out a body-bag on a stretcher through the front door. Detective Chief Inspector McQuiston, the officer in charge, stepped directly into Jardine and Jackie Reid's path. 'Will you get back, please,' he snapped at them testily.

Officious bastard, Jardine thought. He fished in his pocket and produced his ID card. 'We're from Glasgow – Maryhill Police Station.' He nodded in the direction of the body-bag as it was carried past. 'Mrs Moore?'

'So what's it to you?' McQuiston demanded curtly, confirming Jardine's initial assessment.

'We came up to interview her,' Jackie told the man.

McQuiston flashed her a brief and dismissive glance. 'Did you now?' he muttered sarcastically. 'About what?'

'We don't really know,' Jackie had to admit. 'She rang earlier saying that she wanted to speak to us.'

McQuiston sneered at her. 'Oh yes? And why should she want to speak to the Glasgow police, eh?'

Jardine was increasingly irritated at the man's attitude. 'Look, it's a long story,' he interrupted. 'Can we just take a look at the body?'

Jardine received the same, smug look from McQuiston. 'Of course you can. After our people have finished with it.'

Jackie Reid let out a little sigh of impatience. Turning away, she strode over to the stretcher, which had been laid on the ground awaiting an ambulance. She bent over it, unzipping the top. McQuiston barked over at her angrily. 'You're out of order – Constable.'

Jackie ignored him. She pulled the zipper down to Mrs Moore's shoulders. Her eyes fell immediately on the single, small wound in the side of the woman's neck. She looked over at Jardine. 'Mike, you'd better come and take a look at this.'

Jardine hurried over, closely pursued by McQuiston. 'Look, I don't know what you two think you're playing at, but you're not going to do it on my patch,' McQuiston complained.

Jardine whirled on him, his patience finally exhausted. 'Now, listen – we have every reason to believe whoever killed Mrs Moore is also responsible for at least three other murders in the Glasgow area.'

McQuiston was slightly rattled, but he still wasn't going to have his authority undermined. 'Then put your information through the proper channels and I'll look at it.'

Jackie Reid had just noticed Roy Moore, seated in the back of one of the police cars. She nudged Jardine, pointing over to the lad. 'That's Roy, the woman's son.'

'We need to talk to him,' Jardine said to McQuiston.

'Then you'll have to wait until we've finished with him,' the man snapped. 'And that may be some time.

This has got all the hallmarks of a domestic, as far as I'm concerned.' He gave Jardine another sneer. 'Now why don't you both go on back to Glasgow and leave us to sort out our own business?'

'Because as far as *I'm* concerned, there's a mass murderer running around Scotland,' Jardine shot straight back at the man. 'And under the circumstances, I don't think it's too much to ask to speak to a possible witness.' He pushed rudely past McQuiston, counting on not being stopped. The bluff worked. McQuiston nodded his reluctant approval to the uniformed officer guarding the police car. Jardine stepped past him and opened the door, allowing Jackie to climb in beside the frightened boy on the back seat.

'Roy – remember me?' Jackie asked, gently. 'I came to see your mother the other day.'

The lad nodded. 'I remember,' he murmured.

'Your mother phoned me this morning,' Jackie went on. 'She told me she wanted to see me again, there was something she wanted to tell me. Now – do you have any idea what it was about?' Roy shook his head dumbly. Jackie tried another tack. 'Listen, Roy – did your mother ever mention a woman called Joan Mathieson to you?'

'Joan?' Roy repeated, stupidly.

McQuiston had come up behind Jardine, pulling him rudely away from the side of the police car. He thrust his head through the open door, addressing Jackie. 'Right, that's it. You're holding up a murder investigation on my patch.'

'Please – just a couple more questions,' Jackie pleaded with him. She turned back to Roy. 'Listen, Roy – were you in the house when your mother phoned me?

Do you have any idea at all what she might have wanted to tell me about?'

McQuiston snorted derisively in her ear. 'Can't you see you're wasting your time? The kid's defective. He doesn't know his arse from Friday.'

It was a judgment which Jackie was reluctantly beginning to accept herself. She began to ease herself out of the car. Roy Moore looked after her sadly. 'That woman . . .' he muttered suddenly.

Jackie looked at him quickly. 'Joan Mathieson?'

The boy nodded. 'Mum didn't tell you the truth about her,' he said hesitantly, as if he felt he was betraying his mother in some way.

'What about her, Roy?' Jackie prompted, with a friendly smile to reassure him that it was all right.

'She used to come here sometimes when we were kids,' Roy went on. 'After my father died. We called her Auntie Joan – but she wasn't a real auntie.'

'What was she, then?' Jackie asked.

The boy shrugged. 'Just a friend of Mum's.'

Jackie regarded him piercingly. 'You say she only came *after* your father died? Are you sure?'

Roy nodded. 'Sure – *right* after.'

McQuiston had lost his cool completely. He reached into the car, grabbing Jackie's arm. 'Right, you've had your questions. Out of that car – now!'

He pulled her out, slamming the door and banging on the roof as a signal to the driver. The car began to pull away, with Roy Moore staring fearfully out of the window at Jackie Reid. Poor little devil, she thought to herself. McQuiston would probably reduce him to a quivering wreck before he was finished. She turned towards the man, glaring at him accusatively. 'That boy is completely harmless and innocent,' she told him. 'The real killer is running around Glasgow somewhere.'

McQuiston's lip curled in a sneer. 'Well thank you both very much for coming all the way up here to help us,' he said. 'Now if you want any more information, just make sure you do it through the proper channels.' He strode away, leaving them standing there.

'Thanks for your help and co-operation,' Jardine called after him, sarcastically. He glanced across at Jackie Reid. 'We'd better get this information back to Taggart,' he suggested.

Chapter Twenty-five

It wasn't exactly standard practice to visit the homes of policemen on suspension, but then there weren't any hard and fast rules against it, either. And, as someone had to speak to the Gibsons to corroborate Martin Adams' alibi, Taggart had taken the task upon himself. The sound of a baby crying could clearly be heard from the front gate.

Rob Gibson was surprised, flustered and more than a little embarrassed, to find him on the doorstep. 'Oh, it's you, sir.'

Taggart nodded. 'Aye, it was the last time I looked. Can I come in?'

'Yes, of course.' Gibson stepped back, allowing Taggart to step over the threshold. His embarrassment came to the fore. 'If you don't mind, sir – we'll have to go into the nursery,' he muttered apologetically. 'I was just rocking the baby to sleep. Michelle's gone out to the shops.'

Somewhat sheepishly, he led the way into the nursery, where the crying infant lay in its cot, squirming fretfully. Gibson began to rock the cot gently from side to side. The baby quietened down. 'He'll be asleep in a moment, sir. Then we can talk,' Gibson apologised again.

Taggart dismissed it with a vague wave of his hand. 'How is he now?' he asked quietly.

Gibson smiled faintly. 'He's fine. The doctors say there's rarely any long-term effects.'

'And you?' Taggart asked, more pointedly.

Gibson shrugged, looking down at the baby with concern, if not affection. 'I'm coming to terms with it. Michelle still adores him, of course.' He paused, looking up at Taggart. 'We've already discussed it and decided to try again, sir. We'll find another clinic and have another one. One that's really ours this time.'

'Good,' Taggart nodded thoughtfully. He was silent for a while. 'You know something, Rob? I always wanted a son,' he murmured finally. 'I've never told this to anyone. We had a daughter, and I love her dearly. But I thought – maybe next time?' He paused to shake his head sadly. 'Och, it wasn't to be.'

It was impossible not to feel sympathy for the man. Everyone at Maryhill Station knew the story of how childbirth had triggered Jean Taggart's paralysis. 'I'm sorry, sir,' Gibson muttered, genuinely.

Taggart nodded. 'Aye, so was I. For a long time.'

There was another long and thoughtful silence. The baby finally settled down into a deep sleep and Gibson stopped rocking the crib. He stepped back quietly. 'We can leave him now,' he whispered to Taggart. He led the way to the living-room, leaving the nursery door ajar.

Once inside the room, Gibson turned, suddenly, to face his superior directly. It was something of a confrontation. 'Sir, is my career in the police force finished, after what happened?' he blurted out.

'I doubt it,' Taggart said, noncommittally, but there was a thin smile on his lips as he spoke.

'I nearly went with them, you know,' Gibson admitted.

Taggart shrugged. 'You'd have been less than human if you hadn't at least thought about it. But thinking and doing are two very different things. The trick is recognising that difference.' Taggart broke off, suddenly realising that he had just given himself the perfect cue into his main reason for calling. 'That's one of the things that bothers me about your friend Martin Adams. Does *he* know the difference?'

Gibson eyed him guardedly. 'Are you asking me for a professional or a personal opinion, sir?'

'Maybe both,' Taggart said, hedging his bets.

Gibson was thoughtful for a while. 'Martin's got a temper, I can't deny that,' he admitted finally. 'But I can't really see him as a multiple killer.'

Taggart digested the young man's opinion with a thoughtful nod. 'He came here last night, I understand? What did he want?'

'Just to talk,' Gibson said. He smiled thinly. 'Suddenly, we've both got a lot more in common than we thought we had.'

'And how did he seem to you?' Taggart asked.

Gibson was about to answer when there was the sound of a key in the front door. Seconds later, Michelle came in, carrying two shopping-bags. She did not seem too pleased to see Taggart, giving him a frosty stare. Taggart weathered it as best he could. He could hardly have expected a rapturous welcome. He was, after all, the man who had placed her husband on suspension. 'Mrs Gibson,' he muttered politely.

Gibson stepped in quickly, attempting to build a bridge over potentially troubled waters. 'DCI Taggart came to ask about Martin coming here last night,' he explained.

Michelle lowered her bags to the floor, confronting Taggart with a challenging stare. 'That's right, he did,' she said firmly. She did not take her eyes off Taggart. 'And while you're holding him in a cell, his wife's at home on her own with a baby on the way,' she added, pointedly.

Taggart found himself forced on to the defensive. For such an attractive, slightly-built woman, Michelle Gibson could be quite formidable. 'Maybe we won't be holding him for much longer,' he muttered. It was not quite a promise, but it seemed to mollify Michelle somewhat. She bent down to pick up her bags again. 'Well, I'll just go and unpack these and I'll make you a cup of tea, Mr Taggart.'

'No – wait,' Taggart said suddenly, remembering something which had been at the back of his mind for days. 'Now I've got you two together, there's something I wanted to ask you.' He stared at them both in turn. 'You met Joan Mathieson at the christening, didn't you?'

Michelle nodded. 'That's right. Cathy asked if she could hold the baby. It seemed quite important to her.'

'And how did she behave?' Taggart went on.

Gibson thought for a few seconds. 'I must admit, she was a wee bit peculiar.'

'How peculiar?' Taggart asked.

Michelle Gibson smiled. 'Actually, we both joked about it afterwards. It was as if the baby had 666 stamped on his forehead.'

'We were just talking about his features,' her husband put in. 'Cathy mentioned that quite a few people had suggested that the baby had my eyes. Her mother looked at him, then stared at me – and then suddenly thrust the baby back in Michelle's arms as though he had the plague.'

'Without a word,' Michelle added. 'Then she shot off like a startled rabbit.'

Gibson looked at Taggart with a reflective expression on his face. 'You know, I've never thought about it until now, sir – but it was as if she knew something. Maybe, having delivered lots of babies, she was able to tell.'

It wasn't a conjecture which Taggart wished to comment on. 'Tell me – did Joan Mathieson meet Dr Millar *before* she went into the church?' he asked.

Gibson thought about it for a while, finally shaking his head. 'No, I'm pretty sure she didn't.' He paused, thinking back again. 'In fact, I'm quite sure she didn't,' he added, much more emphatically.

Taggart's face was creased in a thoughtful frown. 'Butterflies,' he muttered finally, absently. Neither Gibson or his wife had the faintest idea what he meant, and Taggart didn't bother to explain.

Chapter Twenty-six

Ruth Millar drove up to the lochside cottage with a sense of foreboding she couldn't quite put her finger on. Stepping out of the car, she looked around, trying to identify anything out of the ordinary. There was nothing immediately apparent. Everything was quiet – perhaps unnaturally so. Out of the corner of her eye, she saw something bobbing in the water, half-concealed under the small jetty. Ruth moved towards it, curious. It was a fishing rod, she realised as she came close. But not just any fishing rod. This particular one happened to be one of Colin's most expensive, and prized, pieces of tackle. The sense of foreboding grew into a quiet, expectant dread. She raised her eyes slowly, staring out over the gently rippling waters of the loch.

The skiff was about thirty yards offshore, upside-down in the water. She had failed to notice it earlier because it had been hidden by the jetty. A sob rose in Ruth's throat. 'Colin – oh, my God!' Hastily kicking off her shoes, Ruth raced along the small jetty, peeling off her jumper as she ran. She took to the icy waters in a flying dive, striking out immediately for the capsized boat with strong, sure strokes. Reaching it, she clung to it for a few seconds, catching her breath. Then, taking in a lungful of air, she pushed herself under the water, ducked beneath the upturned boat and surfaced again inside it. Treading water, she peered around in the gloom and was almost relieved to see that it was empty. The thought of coming face to face with Colin's lifeless corpse had been very much in her mind.

She dived back under the surface again, coming up by the side of the skiff and hauling herself up over its bottom, scanning the waters slowly from side to side and then back again. Nothing moved except the faint breeze making patterns on the water. Feeling utterly hopeless, she turned back towards the shore and swam back wearily to the jetty. Reaching land again, she turned and stood gazing frantically out over the loch again for a long time, feeling despair soaking into her mind and body like a numbing drug. Finally, knowing that there was no more she could do, she turned in the direction of the cottage and stumbled, shivering and sobbing, towards the door.

Colin Millar sat on a plain wooden chair, huddled over a blazing log fire. He had changed out of his sodden clothes and put on a dry dressing-gown, but his hair was still wet. He did not look round as Ruth walked in. Relief came over her so fiercely that it was almost anger. 'Damn you, Colin – I thought you were dead,' she spat out at him.

Millar turned to face her at last. He was pale but strangely composed. The expression on his face reminded Ruth of a scolded child. 'I tried to drown myself,' he murmured distantly. 'I thought I'd make it look like an accident – for the insurance.' He broke off, nodding up at the mantelpiece above the fire, where a white envelope was propped up against the wall. 'I wrote you a letter and everything. Only I didn't have the guts to go through with it.'

Ruth walked up beside him, displaying her soaking body to him. 'My God, Colin – I *swam* out there to rescue you,' she told him, accusingly.

Millar hung his head in shame. 'I'm sorry,' he muttered.

Ruth shuddered with exasperation. She moved away to peel off her wet clothes and wrap herself in a warm, dry blanket. Returning, she sat down on the floor in front of the fire, staring into the crackling flames in complete silence for a long time.

'Why?' she demanded finally, looking up at him.

Millar shook his head distractedly. 'You wouldn't understand,' he told her. It was hardly an explanation.

Ruth looked at him thoughtfully. 'Was it the thought of prison?' she asked eventually. She racked her brains for something positive to say, some words of comfort. 'Even if it was for two or three years, Colin – it wouldn't kill you.'

Millar shook his head again, looking up at her. 'Even a single day, Ruth. I can't stand to even think about being locked in. All my life, it's been one of my greatest fears.' He lowered his eyes again. 'But that's not the only reason.'

Ruth stared at him in sheer incomprehension, struggling to understand him. 'Yet you went ahead and did what you did, Colin? Surely you must have realised that you'd be found out one day – that you couldn't get away with it forever?'

Millar smiled wistfully at her. 'Poor Ruth,' he murmured. 'There are so many things about me that you can't understand. So many things you don't even know.'

Anger blazed in Ruth's eyes again for a second. 'Dammit, Colin – I've spent the best part of a week trying to come to terms with the things I *do* know.'

Millar gestured to the early edition of the evening paper lying on the nearby coffee table. 'And now I have that on my conscience as well.' Ruth glanced at the paper, scanning the headline. 'CITY ARCHITECT DETAINED IN MURDER ENQUIRY'. 'They're holding Cathy's husband,' Millar said miserably. 'They don't actually name him, of course, just "an architect" – but it's obvious.' He paused, sighing deeply. 'If they charge him, she'll be left all alone – with my child.' Millar's face screwed up into a look of anguish. 'I couldn't stand to face that, Ruth. I think that's what finally did it.'

Ruth was still regarding him with total bewilderment. 'Over one woman? Why just her?'

Millar sighed hopelessly. 'You still don't understand. How could you?' he muttered.

'Colin, I'm *trying* to,' Ruth shot back. She stared at him sullenly. 'Do you know what our friends are saying about me? I'm the woman so unable to have children that her husband had to impregnate sixty others. God knows, I'm trying.'

'If that's what they're saying, then they're not really our friends,' Millar said. He sounded quite indignant, even slightly pompous.

It was such a ridiculous response that Ruth found it

actually quite amusing. There was the trace of a smile on her face. 'Anyone would think that you were the aggrieved party in all this, Colin,' she observed. It took something of an effort to force herself to become serious again. 'Look, if you feel so badly about Cathy, perhaps there's some way you can try to make it up to her. Perhaps financial – I don't know. Maybe you could go and see her.'

Millar nodded thoughtfully. 'Yes, perhaps I could.'

A sense of the utterly ridiculous began to sweep over Ruth again. For no apparent reason, she found an inane grin forming on her face, a wave of savage, ironic humour invading her mind. 'Maybe you'll have to pay them all financial support,' she observed, beginning to giggle. 'They might have to open a whole new branch of the Child Support Agency just to handle your case.'

The faintest ghost of a smile tugged at the corner of Millar's mouth as he snatched desperately at some light relief in his misery. 'Perhaps they will,' he agreed.

'Let's just hope you don't have to pay all their school fees,' Ruth put in, struggling to repress the bubbling, nervous laughter rising in her throat.

'Or buy them all birthday presents,' Millar added, throwing himself into the ridiculous game. They stared at each other like a pair of drunks, momentarily high on the forced humour which had managed to penetrate the full gloom and tragedy of the situation.

Chapter Twenty-seven

Taggart was studying the photo album rescued from Joan Mathieson's house as Jardine and Jackie Reid arrived back from their trip to Oban. 'So – you didn't arrive in time?' he said, glancing up.

Jardine looked at him in surprise. 'How did you know, sir?'

Taggart put on one of his infuriating 'I know something that you don't know' looks. 'I had a telephone call from one Detective Chief Inspector McQuiston,' he said flatly. 'Not a happy man, was our Mr McQuiston.'

Jardine studied Taggart's face closely, trying to gauge the man's mood. As ever, it wasn't easy. Outwardly, Taggart didn't seem too concerned – in fact he looked somewhat preoccupied with something else. But was he expecting some sort of an apology? Jardine wondered. If so, then he was going to be disappointed, he decided finally. 'He was an arrogant bastard,' Jardine muttered, using attack as a form of defence.

Taggart nodded absently. 'Aye, he sounded it on the phone.'

That appeared to be the end of it, Jardine thought. He wondered, briefly, what Taggart had said to the man, but knew better than to ask. 'Anyway, we did find out one important thing,' he announced, glad to be able to change the subject. 'Agnes Moore, the Oban woman, had a definite connection to Joan Mathieson. The two women knew each other, a long time back. They had a lot in common. Both had large families, and both lost their husbands.'

'Mislaid might be the better word,' Taggart said mysteriously. 'And I think that you'll soon discover that they had one more rather important thing in common, as well.'

'Soon, sir?' Jackie Reid asked.

Taggart nodded, still not giving anything away. 'I'm just waiting for something to come back from Forensic. Should be any minute now.'

'You have remembered that you've got a christening to go to, haven't you, sir?' Jackie asked.

Taggart dismissed it with a wave of his hand. 'Plenty of time for that. In the meantime, let's all play a little game, shall we?'

He was tantalising them deliberately, Jardine realised, but for the moment at least, they had little choice but to go along with it. 'What's the name of the game, sir?' he asked.

Taggart grinned. 'Happy Families,' he announced. He picked up the photo album and a packet of drawing pins and stood up, carrying them across to the notice-board where Jackie Reid had pinned up the pictures of Millar's multiple offspring. 'Right – what did I tell you?' Taggart said. 'This had all the hallmarks of a domestic, right from the start. A family murder.'

'I thought that was what we told you, sir,' Jardine pointed out, but Taggart wasn't really listening.

'And we weren't wrong,' he went on. 'This was a family murder, right enough.' He began to detach photographs from the album, pinning them into place on the notice-board. The first photograph was of a very young Ian Mathieson.

Cathy was glad of her brother's company, although she felt a little guilty about soaking up his sympathy when he had his own worries, and his own reasons to grieve. Just as she had always managed to remain on reasonably familiar terms with her mother, so Ian had shared an especially close relationship with Uncle Tom. Now that the man was gone, Ian must be feeling very vulnerable and very lonely, Cathy thought, because for him, there was nobody else. To the best of her knowledge, Ian had never even had a girlfriend, let alone a close relationship of any kind. He had always been the same, even as a boy. Shy, withdrawn, a loner. Yet with a quiet, inner strength – just as he was demonstrating now. He was with her, not because *he* was lonely, but because he felt that she needed him. And Cathy *had* needed comforting – her strained eyes and tearstained cheeks testified to that.

Ian hugged his sister's shoulders tightly. 'Don't worry, Cathy. If anything happens to Martin, we'll bring the baby up together,' he promised her. He forced a smile for her benefit. 'I'll be the best uncle a kid ever had, you'll see. It'll be like when we were children and I used to pretend I was Dad – remember?'

Cathy did remember, and the memory brought a real smile to her face. She grasped his hand, squeezing it fondly. 'Oh, Ian – I don't know what I'd do without you,' she murmured lovingly.

He grinned sheepishly. 'I know I've always been . . . like the failure of the family – but it will be different now.'

Cathy looked up at him, denial in her eyes. 'You've never been a failure, Ian.'

He shrugged. 'Well, Mum always thought so.'

'In Mum's eyes, we were all failures,' Cathy observed sadly. The thought of her mother brought the tears prickling out in her eyes once more.

Ian found a slightly grubby handkerchief in his pocket, handing it to her. 'Here, dry your eyes,' he told her. 'You need a bit of looking after.' He thought for a second. 'Have you eaten today?'

Cathy shook her head. 'I didn't really feel like anything. And anyway, I couldn't be bothered,' she added.

Ian nodded knowingly. 'That's more the truth. Look – why don't I nip out and get us a nice Chinese takeaway? You've got to eat, you know – you're feeding two now, don't forget.'

Cathy didn't need to really consider the question. She hadn't realised quite how hungry she really was. She nodded enthusiastically. 'That would be nice.'

'Good.' Ian seemed pleased that he had been able to do something practical. He stood up, checking the money in his back pocket. 'I'll go to the Lotus House,' he announced. 'A couple of their Far East Specials should do us a treat.'

'And a spring roll,' Cathy put in, suddenly craving for a Chinese feast.

Ian stooped to kiss her on the forehead. 'And a spring roll,' he confirmed. He turned towards the door. 'Right, you have a little rest and I'll be back in about twenty minutes.' He let himself out of the front door, closing it behind him. Reaching the gate, he stepped out on to the pavement and began to walk down the road, unaware that he was being watched from a car parked across the other side of the street.

Ruth Millar had changed into clean, dry clothes, hanging her wet ones over the back of a chair by the fire. She crossed to the music centre, slipping in a tape of Vivaldi's *The Four Seasons*. As the music swelled out, she returned to her easy chair in front of the fire, preparing to relax and attempt to put all thoughts of Colin out of her mind.

He had seized upon her suggestion to go and see Cathy, even though she had regretted making it as soon as the words left her mouth. In retrospect, it had been a stupid thing to suggest, but she hadn't been thinking clearly at the time. Considering it now, Ruth couldn't help wondering what sort of a reception he was likely to receive. It would hardly be a rapturous welcome, if she admitted him to the house at all. But it had given him something to do, and Ruth was not sorry to have a little time to herself.

Just before she sat down, her eyes strayed to the mantelpiece, and the sealed envelope which Colin had left there. Ruth smiled to herself. How like Colin, she thought. He never seemed capable of thinking through the consequences of his own actions. He even forgot to remove his own suicide note. She stepped towards the mantelpiece, picking up the letter and preparing to toss it into the fire.

The envelope was bulky and quite heavy. Far more than just a note, Ruth reflected. Her eyes took in the inscription written carefully on the front of the envelope in Colin's flowing italic handwriting. 'To my darling Ruth.'

She paused in the very action of consigning the letter to the flames, her curiosity getting the better of her. Retreating to her chair, she sat down, opened the envelope and drew out the carefully folded sheets of paper, beginning to read. She skipped through the first two or three paragraphs, speed-reading without really taking anything in. It was, as she had been expecting, a rambling and apologetic preamble to the stream of maudlin self-pity which would undoubtedly follow.

Only it didn't. The letter suddenly took on a new tone, one that she could never have expected. It was defiant now, rather than apologetic. A detailed and damning confession of one man's life, one man's sins. Suddenly, Ruth's eyes were no longer merely scanning the text, she was reading it with total concentration. Individual words leapt off the pages at her, burning into her mind. Fascinated, horrified and unable to believe the evidence of her own eyes, Ruth forced herself to continue reading the letter. Her hands were beginning to tremble. There was a feeling of tightness in her chest and throat. The fire in front of her suddenly seemed to have lost its warmth.

Finally, Ruth lowered the final page and let the letter drop from her numbed fingers to the floor. Her face was ashen white, her heart pounding inside her breast like a steam hammer. 'Oh my God,' Ruth Millar breathed, fighting to control an urge to scream out at the top of her voice.

Chapter Twenty-eight

Relaxation was impossible. Cathy pushed herself awkwardly to her feet, waddling around the room aimlessly. It was as if, with the birth so near now, her mind kept nagging her body to be on its feet, mobile – and ready. She crossed to the glass of the conservatory, gazing in at the fluttering butterflies for a few moments. They too seemed to need to be constantly on the move, in a constant state of readiness for flight.

Cathy's eyes, sore from so much crying over the past two or three days, were especially sensitive to the bright sunlight which came streaming in to the living-room from the conservatory. Taking a last glimpse at the butterflies, she drew the curtains across, reducing the room to a comfortable state of shade. She began to move towards the kitchen to lay out plates in readiness for Ian's return.

The doorbell rang, stopping her in her tracks. She hesitated in answering, aware that she was not expecting any visitors. It could not be Ian back so soon, for it was less than two minutes since he had left. The Lotus House was a good ten minutes' walk away, and allowing time to wait for the order, he could not possibly be back in less than another twenty-five.

The bell rang again. Hoping that it would not turn out to be two identically dressed clones from the Church of Latter-Day Saints, Cathy lumbered across the room to answer the door. An entire army of Mormons might have been preferable callers. Cathy gaped at the figure of Colin Millar on her doorstep, temporarily dumbfounded by the sheer gall of the man in coming to her home.

He smiled at her sheepishly, feeling as awkward as she did. 'Hello Cathy. Look – do you mind if I come in?'

Cathy was frozen in indecision, her mind a swirling maelstrom of mixed emotions. This man, who had brought so much misery and pain into her life, was also the father of the baby she carried in her womb.

Perhaps Millar sensed this. 'I really need to talk to you – it's about the baby,' he went on.

Almost against her will, Cathy took a step backwards. It wasn't exactly an invitation, but Millar took it as such anyway. He stepped forward over the threshold, slowly closing the door behind him.

'I had to come to see you,' he explained. 'Partly to say how sorry I am that Martin's been arrested – but mostly because I was worried about you, with the baby so close now. This must be a very trying time for you.'

In any other circumstances, Cathy might have

found the enormity of that understatement amusing. As it was, she found his concern – whether it was feigned or genuine – almost offensive. 'My God, but you've got a nerve, coming here,' she breathed.

Millar shrugged, looking slightly apologetic. 'I made sure you'd be alone,' he admitted. 'I waited outside the house until I saw your brother leave.'

'You'd better sit down,' Cathy muttered, grudgingly. The man had obviously taken a lot of trouble to come and see her, and he seemed to have something important he needed to say to her. Despite what he had done to her, Cathy felt that she at least owed him the chance to apologise.

'Thank you.' Millar crossed to a chair and lowered himself into it. He stared up at her nervously, clearly still far from comfortable. 'One of the main reasons I came was to say that if there's anything I can do – anything financial, by way of compensation . . .'

It took a few seconds to sink in, but when it did, Cathy regarded the man with a look of stunned disbelief. 'You've come here to offer me *money*, Dr Millar? You want to buy yourself out of this mess?'

Millar was not prepared for the violence of her reaction. He looked confused, ashamed – even hurt. 'No, please, that's not what I meant. You don't understand.'

Perversely, Cathy found herself feeling almost sorry for the man. 'Then what did you mean, Dr Millar?'

Millar folded his hands in his lap, taking a breath. 'It's just that – if Martin goes to prison – you'll need something.'

'I hear you're quite likely to go to prison yourself,' Cathy pointed out.

Millar nodded absently. 'Yes, perhaps – only for a few years. But I have capital, you see – and I want to make up for what I've done in some way.' He stared at her abjectly, begging her forgiveness. Cathy was silent for several seconds.

'Why me?' she wanted to know finally.

'Because you'll be all alone. And because I feel responsible,' Millar murmured.

Taggart had finished pinning up the photographs of all the children in the Mathieson family, under the pictures of Millar's sixty offspring. He stepped back from the notice-board with something of a grand gesture, allowing Jardine and Jackie Reid to study the display more closely.

The beginnings of understanding showed on Jackie Reid's face. Her mouth dropped slightly open. 'Oh, my God!'

Taggart nodded at her. 'Exactly,' he muttered. His voice was grave, although the faintest hint of triumph still showed through. 'The sixty children of Dr Millar. Joan Mathieson's four children. Note the strong family resemblance.'

The desk sergeant came into the office at that moment, holding a large brown envelope in his hand. He approached Taggart. 'This was just delivered for you, sir.'

'Thanks,' Taggart said, taking the envelope but not opening it. He returned his attention to Jardine, who was studying the photographs on the notice-board with the same shocked expression as Jackie Reid. The penny had just dropped for him as well. 'So we're talking about bigamy as well as everything else?' Jardine said, spelling it out. 'Our Dr Millar had been a busy little man over the years, hasn't he?'

Taggart shook his head. 'Oh, it gets even better, Michael.' He opened the envelope in his hand and started to pull out another photograph. 'I had Forensic do a computer enhancement of the man in the newspaper clipping DC Reid found in Joan Mathieson's house. I asked them to brush out the beard, change the hairstyle and age his face about twenty years. I think the result might surprise you.' He produced the photograph with a flourish, stabbing it into the notice-board with a pin. 'And guess who's been a very naughty boy indeed?'

Jardine whistled through his teeth. Coming on top of Taggart's other revelations, this latest surprise was not so much of a bombshell as an aftershock. Aided by state-of-the-art technology, the grainy newspaper picture of the supposedly drowned sailor in Oban had been transformed into the unmistakable face of Colin Millar. 'A triple bigamist,' Jardine said, revising his earlier conclusion.

Taggart nodded. 'Mathieson... Moore... and Millar. Our good doctor certainly got around a bit.'

'So Joan Mathieson must have recognised him – from the original newspaper cutting,' Jackie put in. 'That's why she went to see Mrs Moore.'

'And both women made a pact – to keep it from their children,' Jardine said, following the deduction through.

'And she recognised him again – in the church, during the Gibson christening,' Taggart added, with a nod. 'It wasn't a butterfly that made her rush out of that church – it was Colin Millar. If there were any butterflies at all, they must have been in his stomach, knowing that he'd been rumbled, after all those years.'

'So he had to get rid of her,' Jackie said. 'He had to kill her so she couldn't spill the beans.'

'And everyone else who might have recognised him once his case went to trial,' Jardine put in. 'No wonder he was worried about the press photographers taking his photo. Once his face appeared in the papers, there were a whole batch of people who might have recognised him.'

Taggart nodded. 'Joan Mathieson's brother Tom, the neighbour who'd known the family, and his second wife. All potential dangers, and all now dead.'

'But why me, sir?' Jackie wanted to know.

'You just happened to be in the wrong place at the wrong time,' Taggart explained. 'All he really wanted to do was to destroy any old photographs of himself which Joan Mathieson might have kept. Of course, he had no way of knowing that she'd already destroyed them herself, many years ago.'

Jackie Reid was silent for a long while, working things through in her mind. 'You realise what this means, sir,' she muttered, in a shocked voice. She turned towards the noticeboard, looking at the photograph of Cathy as a young girl.

'Aye,' Taggart sighed heavily. 'Cathy Adams is pregnant by her own natural father. That's why you're going to have to explain it to her very, very gently.'

Chapter Twenty-nine

'This is a nice house,' Millar said conversationally. 'You and Martin must be very proud of it.'

'Yes, we are,' Cathy nodded absently, wondering when the man was going to leave. She couldn't really understand why he continued to hang around. He appeared to have said his piece, in offering her money, and she thought she had made it quite clear that any such attempt at compensation was neither necessary nor welcome. Yet he showed no signs of preparing to leave. Perhaps there was something more he needed to say.

'Look, would you like a cup of tea, Dr Millar?' Cathy asked, more out of desperation than politeness. It would at least give her a chance to get out of the strained atmosphere of the living-room, and stall for a few more minutes until Ian got back.

Millar nodded. 'Yes, I'd love one.' He pushed himself to his feet. 'I'll just go and look at the butterflies, if I may.' He walked across to the conservatory as Cathy left to go to the kitchen. He pulled back the curtains, staring through the glass wall at the dancing insects with a faint, wistful smile on his face. It froze, suddenly, as he realised his mistake, hardening into a grim mask. Instinct, rather than sound, told him that Cathy had returned from the kitchen and was standing directly behind him.

'Dr Millar – how did you know about the butterflies?' she asked, in a quiet, curious voice.

Millar did not turn to face her, continuing to stare blankly through the glass. 'I saw them as I came in,' he muttered.

'But I shut the curtains just a few seconds before you rang the doorbell.' The first stirrings of doubt had crept into Cathy's voice, the very statement carrying a note of suspicion.

Millar turned, slowly, towards her. 'Then you and Martin must have told me about them,' he said, forcing a smile on to his face.

Cathy shook her head slowly, an expression of doubt and confusion on her face. 'We never mentioned them – either of us, I'm sure.'

Millar shrugged. 'Then I must have read about it in the papers,' he suggested. His increasing desperation showed on his face. It was this, along with another disquieting thought which had just struck her, that made Cathy take a step backwards, the beginnings of fear showing in her eyes.

'And how did you know that Ian was my brother?' she stammered out. 'You said to me – "I waited outside the house until I saw your brother leave". Why should you just assume he was my brother?'

Cathy eyed Millar fearfully as he took a single step towards her. 'Please Cathy – don't press me,' he pleaded with her.

She fell back, increasingly panicky as her doubts began to assume the cold terror of certainty. 'You couldn't know about the butterflies – unless you'd been in this house before,' she breathed.

Millar jumped forward, suddenly seizing her and pinning her arms to her sides. 'Cathy, please – I only came here to help you. I don't want to hurt you, I swear. Don't make me.'

Cathy's eyes were wide open with fear now. She struggled to free herself, but Millar held her securely, and she felt suddenly very weak indeed. Her breathing was erratic, coming in short, deep pants, and her face and neck felt as though they were on fire. A sudden, sharp and cramping pain knifed through her lower abdomen, causing her to clench her teeth. 'Why?' she managed to hiss out, still not understanding.

Millar's face was torn with anguish. He didn't really need to be a doctor to realise that Cathy was going into labour. His daughter was about to give birth to his child – and he could not afford to let either of them live. Tears welled up in his eyes. He dropped his arms from Cathy's shoulders, knowing that she could no longer struggle against him or run away.

'She recognised me . . . your mother. In the church. I didn't have any choice, Cathy – don't you see that? Everything would have come out. I was a bigamist, you see.'

A second wave of contractions tore at Cathy's body. Freed from Millar's grip, she staggered backwards and collapsed upon the settee, staring up at him in horror as the final and chilling revelation sank home.

'Oh my God. You're my father!' she screamed out at him. For that one moment, the loathing and revulsion in her voice drowned out the fear.

Deep, racking sobs shook Millar's body. He was weeping openly now, all his guilt, his regrets and his pain just pouring out of him. 'I swear I didn't know when you walked into my clinic,' he blurted out. 'I had no idea. It wasn't until later – when I saw your mother. I'm sorry, Cathy. I'm so sorry.'

Another shorter, but more excruciating pain spasm caused Cathy to scream out in agony. Through eyes misted and blurred with pain and tears, she watched Millar strip off his tie and stretch it out between his hands like a garotte.

He moved towards her, kneeling at the foot of the settee. 'Oh God, Cathy. I'm so desperately sorry,' he sobbed, leaning forward to press the tie against her throat.

Cathy's last thought was not for her own life, but for the new life she was about to bring forth. 'Please help my baby,' she croaked weakly, before the taut material dug into her windpipe, cutting off even her final scream of parturition.

'Stop it, Colin. It's over – finished.'

Ruth Millar's voice was icily cold, and imperative. Millar whirled round, to find his wife standing by the open inner door of the butterfly conservatory, his letter in her hand. He rose slowly to his feet, still holding the outstretched tie in his hands. On the settee, Cathy gagged, coughed, and began to make a series of low moaning sounds.

Millar turned fully to face Ruth, taking a step towards her. She held his eyes in a cold, challenging stare, freezing him in his tracks. 'Me as well, Colin?

You'd murder your own daughter, your grandchild, your wife?' The hate blazing in her eyes was softened, momentarily, by a flash of pity. 'You fool, Colin – you poor, weak, useless fool.' Millar's shoulders slumped. The tie slipped from his fingers to the floor. He sank to his knees on the carpet, blubbing like a child. Ruth stepped past him, not even bothering to look down at his wretched form. 'It's too late for your tears, Colin,' she muttered coldly, as she moved towards Cathy.

Cathy began to wail, and scream, and moan, as Ruth moved purposefully towards her. The dreadful sound rose in intensity until it filled the room.

'Ian Mathieson was just turning the corner of the street carrying the bag of takeaway food as Jardine and Jackie Reid climbed out of their car. They paused by the gate, waiting for him. He eyed them both uncertainly. 'Why are you here?'

Jardine's face was grim. 'We have to speak to your sister, Ian. And you, as a matter of fact. I'm afraid we have some rather shocking news.'

Jackie Reid tugged at Jardine's sleeve suddenly, urgently, forcing his attention. She pointed to the blue Ford Probe parked a few yards down the road. 'Mike – isn't that Dr Millar's car?'

Almost simultaneously, a shrill and piercing scream came from the house. Ian Mathieson dropped the bag of Chinese food on the pavement, shock registering on his face. 'Oh God – Cathy,' he blurted out, breaking into a run up the drive towards the front door. Jardine and Jackie were only inches behind him. They both pushed roughly past him as he opened the door, jumping into the house. The wailing cries were coming from one of the upstairs bedrooms. Jardine bounded up the stairs two at a time, with Jackie close on his heels. Following the sound, they both burst into the main bedroom.

Their first sight was of Cathy lying on the bed, her clothing hastily ripped away from her body and strewn around the floor. The sheets and mattress of the bed were soaked with bright, fresh blood. She was silent and unmoving. The screaming continued, echoing around the apparently empty room. Then Ruth Millar stepped out from the en-suite bathroom, cradling a screaming, newly-born infant in her arms. She glanced only briefly at Jardine, Jackie Reid and Ian before walking over to the bed and laying the squawling baby across Cathy's breast. The girl's arms came up, weakly but gratefully, to hug the baby gently against her.

Ruth Millar turned back to Jardine and Jackie. 'You'll want my husband,' she murmured calmly. 'He's downstairs.' She looked at Ian. 'And I think your sister needs you right now.'

Ian rushed to Cathy's side, kneeling down beside the bed. He began to stroke her forehead, gently, lovingly.

Jardine and Jackie exchanged a silent glance, knowing that they were not needed. They backed out of the bedroom and began to walk down the stairs.

Millar sat in the conservatory, on the wall beside the mud pool. Bright, colourful butterflies danced around his head in an aerial ballet. Millar glanced up as he heard them enter, a sad little smile on his face. 'It's a shame to see them locked up, isn't it?' he asked. 'They should be free . . . we all should be free.'

Jardine stepped forward to confront the man directly, adopting a stern, businesslike expression. 'Dr Colin Millar – I must caution you – '

Millar cut him short with a little wave of his hand. 'I know, I don't have to say anything. But I'd like to talk, if you don't mind. I have rather a lot to say, you see. I'm not afraid any more.' He paused as a richly coloured swallowtail butterfly alighted on his knee. He admired it for a few seconds, until it finally fluttered off again. Then he rose slowly to his feet, smiling wistfully at Jardine and Jackie. 'You know – the strongest cages are the ones we make for ourselves,' he murmured, taking a step towards them.

Chapter Thirty

With uncharacteristic generosity, Superintendent McVitie had brought out a bottle of Scotch to celebrate the end of yet another case. He poured drinks for Taggart, Jardine and Jackie Reid, raising his own glass in a toast. 'Well done – all of you,' he said.

Jackie Reid was looking at the notice-board, with all the pictures of Millar's children. 'It's not over for them, though – is it?' she observed. 'I can't help wondering just how many lives that man has ruined.'

McVitie walked over to join her, also studying the photographs. 'Let's just pray that they don't all turn out like their father,' he said sombrely. 'Otherwise we'll have the biggest crime wave this city's ever seen.'

Jardine regarded his superior curiously, not sure

whether the man was joking or not. McVitie was not usually known for his sense of humour.

The telephone rang. McVitie snatched it up, listened for a few seconds and nodded over to Taggart. 'Jim, it's Jean, for you. She seems rather upset about something.'

Taggart slapped his forehead with the flat of his hand. 'The christening,' he blurted out. 'I completely forgot.' He looked over at Jardine, slight panic registering on his face. 'What time is it?'

Jardine grinned. 'Time you were at the church, sir.'

Taggart scowled at him. 'It's all right for you to joke about it,' he complained. 'Think of my problems. What's worse – having a godson named Xavier, or the fact that he's the son of a mass murderer?'

'Having to tell Livingstone, I should think,' Jardine pointed out.

Taggart looked at his young colleague thoughtfully for a second, finally nodding. 'Aye, you're right.' He stepped across to McVitie, taking the telephone out of his hand. 'Hello, Jean? Look, I'm sorry but I got held up. I'll be there in about fifteen minutes. In the meantime, there's something I want you to break to Peter for me. You'll be good at it.'

Jean Taggart listened with mounting horror as her husband explained the situation to her. She glanced nervously around, acutely aware that Peter Livingstone was only a few feet away from her. She held the telephone receiver close to her mouth, trying to muffle her words by cupping her hand around the mouthpiece. 'I can't tell him *that*,' she hissed into the phone. 'It will absolutely devastate him.'

The ploy failed to work. Livingstone hurried to her

side, a worried look on his face. 'What is it? What will devastate me?' he demanded. He lifted the phone from Jean's hands. 'Hello, Jim? What's going on? What will devastate me?'

Taggart thrust the telephone into Jardine's hands, making a beeline for the office door.

The surprise move caught Jardine completely off guard. Left, figuratively, holding the baby, he could only mutter nervously into the telephone as a distraught Peter Livingstone continued to demand an explanation.

'Oh, Peter – it's me, Mike Jardine. Sorry, but Jim just left. He said Jean would explain everything to you. Sorry, but I don't know any more.' Jardine slammed the phone back into its cradle. Glaring angrily, he rushed out of the office in pursuit of Taggart, catching up with him in the corridor. 'That was a cowardly thing to do, sir,' he said accusingly.

Taggart faced him squarely, unrepentant. 'It's called delegation. Besides – maybe I just feel I've already done my share.' He turned and walked away down the corridor, pausing at the door and looking back. 'Oh, and Peter . . .'

'I'm Mike, sir,' Jardine reminded him.

Taggart nodded absently. 'So you are.' He walked back to Jardine slowly, clapping a hand on the young man's shoulder. 'Tell me honestly, Michael – do you think this will affect my street credibility?'

Despite himself, Jardine had to smile. 'Your street cred, sir? I think this'll make it.'

Taggart nodded thoughtfully. 'Aye, maybe it will,' he muttered finally. He turned away again, hurrying off to the christening with a renewed sense of pride.